AF575736

BEST CANADIAN STORIES 2026

EDITED BY ZSUZSI GARTNER

Biblioasis
Windsor, Ontario

FIRST EDITION

ISBN 978-1-77196-678-8 (Trade Paper)
ISBN 978-1-77196-679-5 (eBook)

Guest edited by Zsuzsi Gartner
Editorial assistant: Ashley Van Elswyk
Copyedited by Jill Ainsley
Series designed and typeset by Ingrid Paulson

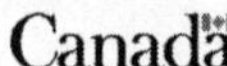

Published with the generous assistance of the Canada Council for the Arts, which last year invested $153 million to bring the arts to Canadians throughout the country, and the financial support of the Government of Canada. Biblioasis also acknowledges the support of the Ontario Arts Council (OAC), an agency of the Government of Ontario, which last year funded 1,709 individual artists and 1,078 organizations in 204 communities across Ontario, for a total of $52.1 million, and the contribution of the Government of Ontario through the Ontario Book Publishing Tax Credit and Ontario Creates.

PRINTED AND BOUND IN CANADA

CONTENTS

Zsuzsi Gartner

INTRODUCTION

Once upon a time, a short-story hunter tasked with seeking out the most wonderful stories in the land from the previous year found herself in a burning boreal forest; in Ceylon before Sri Lanka was Sri Lanka; inside a computer game in eighteenth-, nineteenth-, and twenty-first-century Quebec; on a freezing mountaintop in Tasmania; in a sweltering monastery in Mexico; and on a barren, unnamed moon. The story hunter watched a woman fall from an opera-theatre balcony, waited for a bull moose behind a pine-beetle blind, and partook of an unconventional Christmas feast. She stalked stories with tranquilizer darts and with a butterfly net, as some stories were as fierce as eight-year-old girls, others as elusive as the scent of moon dust. She hunched next to mountain streams scooping stories by hand like a grizzly scoops salmon, tossing back the fry too undeveloped yet to satisfy her vast appetites.

Many of these marvels were not easy to find, hidden as they were amidst the forests of sameness and swamplands of meh. The cities and suburbs and ex-urbs hid stories as well. The story hunter donned mufti and went knocking door to door to find the stories inside houses where the air was crisped to sixty-four degrees while temperatures blistered outside, houses where detoxing teens oozed drugs through their pores, houses divided into apartments where the online world was more satisfying than anything IRL, and apartments in a nineteenth-century heritage building set ablaze.

Like the naturalists and scientific explorers of the Victorian era, the story hunter discovered new lexicons: the ciphers of amateur cyber cryptographers, the close parsing of CNN.com and *NYT* required of aspirational newcomers to Manhattan, the deceptively simple language of gaming commands, the nonlinear communication style of the Intergalactic Federation of Research Camaraderie, the coded meanings of emojis, and the lingua franca of children wielding their otherworldly power at the beach: *Boomshaka. Lingwalla. Boomwalla!*

Boomwalla, indeed! The story hunter had tumbled down a rabbit hole and was surrounded by an eclectic array of stories all deserving her full attention, like Alice in the midst of her furred and feathered coterie. And like the Dodo after the mad Caucus-race, the story hunter determined that all were winners and all must have prizes. She hopes the authors will accept these accolades in lieu of sugary confections and a thimble.

*

It seems fitting to the story hunter as she sits sweating in her lair during the year's first—and very early—heat wave, tranquilizer gun and butterfly net hung up on the back wall, that the first and last stories in this anthology blaze with the urgency of the climate crisis. Rishi Midha's "We Are Busy Being Alive" is a crisply told tale of suburban and familial anxiety amid a sweltering heat wave, a cheeky yet tender take on Tolstoy's truism that every unhappy family is unhappy in its unique way. "What Burns," a tour de force of incandescent prose by Julie Bouchard, translated by Arielle Aaronson, involves multiple conflagrations—of forests, of a building, of souls. This story is afire on so many levels that it's a heat source unto itself.

It was a rare pleasure to chance upon excellent stories set in the historical past, as these are few and far between in short fiction. The deeply moving and quixotic journey of Critchley Parker Jr, a historical figure, in Aaron Kreuter's "On Tasmanian Shores" recalls Jim Shepard, the American author who has crafted so many riveting historically located stories. Both a love story and a tale of political idealism, "On Tasmanian Shores" echoes from the past into our uniquely fraught present. In Grant Buday's "The Light Never Shuts Up," the benighted Miroslav, who carved gravestones and monuments back home in Bratislava, is cast upon the shores of early twentieth-century Acapulco. This is Voltaire's *Candide* on the head of a pin—a nimble story of one man's alternating bad luck and good luck, with an ending shot through with grace. D. F. McCourt's "One Way Out," a captivating narrative set in eighteenth- and nineteenth-century Quebec and imbued with tragic and mystical elements, takes place within a computer game, which itself is a kind of metafiction. A story within a story (within a story) and, within each, devastatingly difficult sacrifices and choices to be made.

"A Language of Shrugs and Sparks" by Kaitlin Ruether uses computer technology to tell a story of dual obsessions, convincingly creating an online world of puzzle-solvers and codebreakers, and an IRL world of sad-girl love. Like the young game creators of Gabrielle Zevin's *Tomorrow, and Tomorrow, and Tomorrow* the characters here are both adorable and heartbreaking in the contrast between their online smarts and their emotional flailings. In "The Formula," a tender-tough story of various addictions, queer relationships, and forgiveness, the humble technology of the emoji is used as a survival mechanism and emotional code. In Alex Leslie's hands the pictographs rise to the level of poetry, like something coaxed from the mind of a Zen monk: *ocean lightbulb boy, shooting-star turtle skull, star waving-hand dog.* Deploying technologies not yet invented, Petra Chambers's "Containment" defies description. A late-twentieth-century coming-of-age story meets academic syllabus by way of the future as formatted through "significant alterations to the software of the interstellar communication matrices" is the best the story hunter can muster. Witty, super smart, moving—it slaps, as the kids might say.

With "Wo" and "Keeping Things Fresh," Randy Boyagoda and Shashi Bhat have found singular ways of telling an oft-told story, both towering above the myriad trope-laden accounts of South Asian newcomers to North America, a CanLit subgenre since the 1970s. Self-deprecating humour is archly wielded in both stories. Reading "Keeping Things Fresh" is like drinking a Bat Bite cocktail, first the light tang of citrus, followed by the darker, weightier undertones of rum. Shashi Bhat's deft satire of contemporary relationships is contained in a moving account of a woman leaving behind her younger world-beating self. Randy Boyagoda's "Wo" is a master class in understatement and dialogue that says little but speaks volumes. After experiencing political and religious graft, and loss, in his native Ceylon, and then the distinction of being "the only brown man in town" in 1960s Canada, Boyagoda's narrator relates his story with tongue firmly in cheek and his eye on the prize.

*

In the past, the story hunter has attempted definitions of a great short story ("A great short story casts a long shadow, and, like Whitman, sings a song of itself, is embedded with the atomic particles of other stories, of stories past and stories yet unwritten, and yet is wholly itself"), but often they were just so much wankery. Much better to borrow from contemporary masters of the form like Lorrie Moore: "A short story is the intersection of the usual and ordinary with the sudden and extraordinary. Short stories are about how the world is not what is seems—the literary equivalent of biodiversity." Moore again: "Part puppet show, part mugging." And the incomparable George Saunders, who has reached guru status when it comes to writing (and teaching about writing) short fiction: "We might think of a story as a system for the transfer of energy. Energy, hopefully, gets made in the early pages and the trick, in the later pages, is to use that energy. Always be escalating."

All the stories in this anthology have reserves of energy to spare, never flagging, never spinning their wheels. And when it comes to the art of escalation a few of them are firing on all cylinders, including "The Light Never Shuts Up," "Jack's Christmas Dinner," "Camouflage and Fame," and "Sand Penis." In Bill Gaston's "Jack's Christmas Dinner," a sorry specimen of roadkill becomes the centrepiece of a Yuletide feast, but not before a series of small escalations that end up bringing a group of near-strangers together. A visceral and pungent version of the European folk tale "Stone Soup," Gaston's unsentimental story is as entertaining as it is moving. In Evan J's slyly titled "Camouflage and Fame," the narrator wants to be the first famous queer hunter but multiple distractions thwart their efforts—Instagram posts, a macho hunter father, an amiable game warden—intruding on the scene like characters that enter without knocking in a sitcom, escalating the coiled tension. Repeated phrases add to the sense of movement, lines that are deceptively simple yet culminate in a powerful incantatory effect. And "Sand Penis." What can be said about a story with a title like that except that it better live up to it? And it does, in aces. Erin MacNair's shimmering, kaleidoscopic, bitingly funny fiction about a children's urban beach outing gone gonzo brightly illuminates the strange power of pre-adolescent girls. George Saunders would applaud.

Caught with her butterfly net are two stories the story hunter finds deliciously elusive, morphing from one thing to another depending on what angle you look at them, like one of those vintage 3-D postcards. They maintain their air of mystery after reading; their wings resist being pinned to the board. They are short in length but long on haunting. In Sophie Crocker's transcendent "Castor & Pollux," all the Geminis of the world are drafted to fight in a "grimy proxy war" in space, sacrificed, à la the fighters in *The Hunger Games*, for the good of those left behind. This touching story seems expansive enough, generous enough, to contain the universe. Margaret Sweatman achieves something equally transcendent with "Sounding a Name." The story evokes St. Petersburg sometime before the war on Ukraine, a city in decay where "everything is in the past, even the future." Through an imperceptible sleight of hand, like a magician's trick, the author tilts the story's perspective from an unhappy poet to a woman who tells him stories but never tells him her name. The reader knows from the audacious opening line what happens to her and still gasps when it finally happens.

*

It is considered sporting at this point for a story hunter to mount a defence of the short story in a world bedazzled by reels depicting what the Disney princesses would look like in "real life," door-stopping, wildly sweeping, multi-generational sagas, and Hallmark-style pensées masquerading as poetry. But the story hunter believes the short story needs no eleventh-hour rescue. The short story is not a damsel bound to the train tracks nor an at-risk species like the North American right whale. The short story is alive and well, whether wild or domesticated. Readers of short fiction, though—there we have a near-extinction-level crisis. What will help swell the ranks of the short-fiction reader? How can conservationists return its population to the robust levels of the short story's golden age when the likes of F. Scott Fitzgerald published stories in glossy magazines ("the slicks") to support his novel-writing and drinking habits? Now there's a problem that bedevils us!

It is also considered cricket for the story hunter to provide a caveat that a different story hunter, one younger or older, thinner or more amply fleshed, balder, bolder, sexier, smarter, one more familiar with Instant Pots or with Sanskrit, one with a different set of chromosomes, one less prone to night sweats, more at home with a Brazilian wax, less enamoured of butter, more sympatico with trash pandas, one armed with a compound crossbow and live-baited traps, would have returned to the palace with a different menagerie of stories. This is not untrue. But, as the enduring and endearing Kurt Vonnegut Jr famously wrote, So it goes.

Rishi Midha

WE ARE BUSY BEING ALIVE

Tommi sits brooding in her fairy-tale chamber beneath the glow of string lights criss-crossing the walls. She knows, from a glance out the window, from the suffocating stillness of the night, that another heatwave is touching down; also from the rattle of the AC straining to keep the mansion cooled to a crisp sixty-four degrees despite doors and windows left open throughout. She has tried to educate her parents on the role of energy consumption in climate change, but it was dismissed as another one of her crusades.

Alone with her principles, she returns to scrolling a feed of friendly faces, ideas shared without friction, and jokes which need not be explained. She switches to an account that indulges her more private interests. Inspiring women who have already made the pledge offer learnings and glimpses into their new lives. The suturing kit in her lap emanates a soft pulse like a newborn. She fingers the tips of needles secured in a row, twirls the threads wound tight around plastic knobs. Each tool is labelled with Mom's neat handwriting.

Before the moment passes, she takes the kit to the bathroom, undresses, sits on the toilet, and with a hand towel clenched between her teeth, begins stitching the skin of her thighs. She carries on until there is a firm resistance when she spreads her legs more than a few fingers' width. The cool sting of the sterilizing pad snaps her out of shock. She showers away the sweat and tears, waddles to bed, and returns to the feed of women she can finally call comrades. She drifts into a righteous sleep, the arguments defending her decision rattling around in her dreams.

At breakfast, Tommi's mother leans against the fridge and watches her from afar. Tommi keeps a low profile, slouched over her cereal. It is a welcome distraction when Jason sprints into the room. He rounds the kitchen table, announcing each lap with a shriek, then ducks beneath the table and trips over his feet, landing directly between Tommi's knees. She comes to moments later, curled up in a ball, coughing cereal milk on to the floor. The hand she produces from between her thighs is wet with blood. Jason runs away screaming and kicks over a house plant.

"It wasn't his fault," Tommi says to her mother, who tends to the torn stitches in the laundry room. She sits above the dryer with her legs open. "Maybe it was his male programming," she muses, chuckling and then wincing. Lounging in that vulnerable position, still stunned from the incident, she feels immersed in her role as the eccentric architect of a fairy tale imposed on the dreary household. She waves her wand and the bloody jeans hanging on the garbage rim fall inside.

Her mother backs away from her groin and promptly starts reorganizing the suturing kit. This time Tommi is not sweating, or in tears, thanks to the Lidocaine numbing her legs and a dose of Ativan reluctantly administered. She wonders how anyone could be so high-strung taking these things on the daily.

"Thanks, Momma! A bonding experience."

She tests her new stitches with an awkward half-squat. Her mother pauses at the door.

"What will you tell your work?"

"Of all the questions, that's the one she asks," Tommi mutters. She locks eyes with her mother and feels fabulously cruel.

*

After dropping Tommi at work, Maxine drives aimlessly through the gated community. Folks sit on shaded porches, watching sprinklers spout water over the spiky St. Augustine grass from a community system that rations out the water every third day between eight and nine. The porch-sitters shift their gaze to her passing car, the movement surpassing slightly the excitement of a sprinkler.

Initially, she was tempted to embrace the attitude of her husband: *Teens will be teens*, he said this morning, before scurrying out the door an hour earlier than he'd ever left for work. But this response too much reminded Maxine of her own parents. *You've emerged from oblivion, well congratulations, we're entering it*, her mother once said, to dismiss a debate with a fiery, teenaged Maxine. She shudders, driving past identical stucco homes, lawns without sidewalks, and a man-made lake dyed turquoise. If oblivion is anywhere, it is here.

Maxine initiates a benevolence meditation, channelling a universal force that merges her hands with the leather of the steering wheel, the rumble of the engine, and the forest surrounds. This is one of many daily activities that constitute a holistic campaign to preserve her well-being and longevity. Without a clue which expert's claims to believe (she has consumed them all), she took the kitchen-sink approach: retinols, fasts, blue-zone diet, ten-mile walks, 4 a.m. wake-ups, cold plunges, and a $100 monthly spend on vitamins and supplements. She recognizes that, beyond her physical maintenance, Tommi is her ticket to the mentality of the youth, the zeitgeist. In exchange for access, Maxine would be Tommi's champion. No—Maxine will be her champion (best to use affirmative language). At book club and oyster Thursday, when the ladies groan about their teenagers, Maxine *will* be the youth's representative. To close the meditation, she recites a brief maxim—*lapses in mindfulness are the root of all your perceived flaws.* In her spellbound moment she allows the car to drift to the shoulder and, before correcting the wheel, runs over a cluster of small turtles. This she does not notice thanks to the suspension of the Range Rover.

Jason, whose head was hanging out the back passenger window to witness the seemingly intentional massacre, immediately starts weeping. Maxine shoos him, smiling absently in the rear-view mirror. "Stop that." He is struggling against the seat belt to turn around. Unbuckling, he faces the rear window. Pockets of melting air create shimmering pools of red on the asphalt. The Florida oaks seem to sag deeper, encroaching on the highway as if in mourning.

Upon reaching home, Maxine has achieved a state of pure connectedness. With faint amusement she watches Jason flock to the backyard, then caresses the garage buzzer and patiently watches the door fold upon itself. Unveiled is a collection of junk larger than she recalls ever having seen. Above it, a layer of dust made grotesquely visible by the sunlight flooding in. Somehow, she has walked past this daily without taking offence.

Titillated by her disgust, and without stepping into the house, she spends the rest of the morning calmly transferring junk to the Range Rover. After hauling it to the landfill, she gets a car wash and vacuums the interior for good measure. Later she naps by the pool in a mesh, bug-protected enclosure with a clear head, letting the obscene heat wash over her, feeling that the day, despite every obstacle, was a success.

*

A car built to hug corners on a track, or meander between coastal towns, sits idle on the I-95. The machine howls with hundreds of other repressed engines in a chorus audible from the coast. Their passengers are shielded from the melting world with air conditioning and sound systems on blast.

Landon welcomes the traffic, which gives him the alone time needed to map out his next move. He hit the freeway at the best possible moment: the congestion is spectacularly awful, as everyone had the same idea to vacate the smog and steel of the city ahead of the heatwave.

The regional train whistles by. Not long ago, he rested his forehead against the train window and watched the frozen mass of cars with disdain. Some years before that, before Jason, he cycled to work from their downtown apartment, Tommi biking at his side en route to school. He is reminded of her complaints about this progression, how excessive their lifestyle has become. Ironically, Landon suspects it was such excess that gave her the space to reflect and decide to be above it. He is not concerned by her argument that he "will never be content." Contentment seems rather dull.

He rewinds the podcast, annoyed at rehashing a debate already resolved. Today's episode deserves his fullest attention. The guest on-air left an executive role at a bank to start the premier e-sports betting platform in the country. Landon revels in his go-to daydream: a talk-show host fawning over his effortless charisma; his friends, who are so disinterested in change, marvelling at his achievements from the other side of a television screen, finally recognizing that their novelties are entirely banal: five-star travel, kids' college admissions, lateral career moves. His infinitely more compelling colleagues on r/alpha and various podcasts, that caste of men who speak in streams of romance, misadventures turned heroic, would welcome him with open arms. They are the engine propelling him towards a sharp corner, which will eventually give him the courage to turn.

But, presently, around the corner is his idyllic suburban home. Maxine's Rover is in the garage, and the space is unusually tidy. He recalibrates in the silence of the car, preparing to pretend to care about whatever attracted Tommi to the stitching thing. Her whims are not a concern—she is smarter than him and Maxine combined. He is inspired by her principles. At fourteen years old, it hardly matters what they are.

*

"How was work, Tommi?" says Maxine, after food is doled out at the dining table.

"Went well! Pretty average day."

Tommi's day did not go well. After arriving late and struggling to ascend the stairs, she was banished to the smoothie stand, the lowliest position at the mall. Some hours later, the AC broke down, and the place where her thighs are knotted together produced an unprecedented quantity of sweat.

"It would *literally* be illegal for them to fire me over a physical limitation," Tommi adds. She scans the room, waiting for anyone to challenge her.

Maxine tries to catch Landon's eye, but he has been distant since learning that several of his prized possessions went to the dump today. She turns to Jason, who pokes at his plate and offers none of his usual entertainments. She watches the thermometer suctioned to the window climb another two degrees despite the descending sun. Finally, she returns her attention to Tommi.

"Tommi, we just wanted to tell you that—"

"Maybe wait until later, Ma," says Tommi, gesturing with her eyes towards Jason.

"Right."

With his plate already empty, Landon says "Wow. Delicious." The two-word feedback he has provided, without fail, for all meals in recent history. "Yes, perfectly cooked, Momma!" Tommi adds. Her plate is empty too. Maxine, who has hardly begun eating, responds with a strained smile. Tommi collects some dishes and waddles away.

After watching Maxine finish her plate, Landon rises wearily from a slouch. "Let's just take it easy on her."

"Actually, I read all about her decision. And I support it," says Maxine, in the most casual tone. It seems to satisfy Landon. He clears the remaining dishes and takes them to the kitchen.

The air of something serious approaching cannot be ignored when the group reconvenes at the table instead of their typical divergence to separate corners of the house. Maxine purses her lips, Tommi basks in the awkwardness, and Landon tries to look indifferent. Jason looks between them with wide eyes.

"Is Jason going upstairs?" Maxine suggests to Landon.

"He's not gonna understand anything. Hell, I probably won't either."

Maxine shuts her eyes and, upon opening them, her expression is resolute.

"Tommi—" she starts, but she is immediately interrupted by Jason, who abandons his silence, drops his trousers, and mounts the dining table. "Adoom-DA! Adoom-DA!" he sings, as he rotates his hips, his tiny penis flopping around at their eye level. Tommi dog whistles and starts a quirky dance of her own. Maxine shrieks and yanks him from the table to wrestle him upstairs. Landon and Tommi are left at the table, delighted by the sudden release. He gives Tommi an inadvertent nod, and Tommi beams back at him. Caught off guard by her flush of enthusiasm, he shrugs and pours himself a bourbon.

*

Tommi's shift is almost over. The janitor circles the food court to clear the overflowing trash bins, mixing the blue, green, and black into a common receptacle since none of them were used correctly. When he arrives at the stand, she smiles and spoons a full tub of fruit from her cart into his. Feeling sorry that their relationship has never made it past that exchange, she asks his name, to which he says Frank. She wishes Frank a wonderful night.

The late afternoon sun beaming through the sunroof sets the marble hall aglow. The AC has not been fixed, but she has settled into the oppressive heat, hardly aware of the discomfort of her rubbing thighs. Frank's cart fades into the gleaming distance. She unlooked for and unprecedented. You will welcome the new world as you do all things, with grace and intelligence.

How do I know this?

Because behind the men and their pits, I hear the river.

Do you hear it, Lynka?

Do you hear it?

Jr.

Kaitlin Ruether

A LANGUAGE OF SHRUGS AND SPARKS

*Update: ***First page of Blastments Decrypted*** [LauraLies]*

We all woke up to that announcement on Friday morning. Had to go do our jobs anyway. It was cruel, really, and I don't think a single person in the codebreaking community got a thing in their real lives done. I know I didn't. UltraTax customers in need of support went unsupported by me—I had more important things to think about.

Like how she had done it.

I must have read Laura's forum post four hundred times that day. I love the way she writes, the humility.

> *"Hi friends! I had an idea last month and ran with it, as I do. We're all obsessive here, but I hadn't been thunked in the head with a new idea in a while. Thank you endlessly to MoneyKiller for helping me run the algorithms. I couldn't*

have done it without her. We have decoded the first page of The Blastments Doctrine, *guys!"*

She always made you feel like you were part of every success. We're all obsessive here. We. Obsessive. We're all here.

She wasn't wrong. My eyes were constantly too dry, blinking rapidly at the computer screen. I was hooked. Like the hundreds of amateur cryptographers glued to the BlueBird puzzles, I wanted to solve one of the internet's most infamous mysteries: decoding the eighty-two-page puzzle called *The Blastments Doctrine*. I wanted to prove my intelligence and creativity and be a part of history, but most of all I wanted to make an impression on Laura. I thought I loved her. Or rather—I made that joke to myself when I got a little too excited. *I'm in love.* She didn't know I existed.

After a few hours of lallygagging, I clocked out of my work-from-home customer support job. Closed one window and opened another. Blinked hard, began tracing the lines of Laura's cribbing and multi-cipher approach. Her revelation worked for one page, but each page used a new encryption style—this was only another clue. I could see what she was doing but not how she had done it. Maybe if I got stoned. When I get high I can almost feel it—the curiosity and obsession that can lead someone to a breakthrough like this. I pulled my eyes from this screen to yet another and sent Matt a message on Signal.

Irl.

Matt told me his birthday once but I forgot it, maybe immediately. What I do remember is that he was kneeling next to his bed, his shaggy reddish hair in his eyes. I was in the bed. I don't remember why this was the arrangement. I think we were both naked.

I had asked him what his sign was and he had scoffed and mimed a man shooting an arrow. It was the summer and I was hot and never slept well in an unfamiliar bed, so it took some thought before I said, "December?" He said, "November," and then a number, but I can't remember what the number was now. Obviously, it was at the end of the month. I know when Sagittarius season is.

After that, he refused to tell me. "I was never born," he said, coy. "How can I have a birthday if I was never born?"

So, anyway, I know that his birthday is coming up, and I know that he will be thirty-one, because despite all this never-born stuff, he did text me last December 1 and announce himself as a thirty-year-old. He did that on purpose so that I wouldn't suss out the actual day. I suppose it's a joke we do now. On December 2 I showed up at his house with a fancy bottle of rum. I love him, and this is important, but he loves someone else and has never hidden this from me. I'm grappling with it. I make do.

Today I poke at what I don't know. "You're going to be aging soon," I say around a cloud of marijuana smoke.

"Twenty-nine," he says proudly.

"Benjamin Button?"

"Something like that."

"You having a party?" I pass the joint back into his waiting fingers.

"George will want to do something."

I feel the smoke in my head, in my mouth, joining me into one flowing object. "Is it weird that I've never met George?"

"Nah," Matt says. "It's fine." He knows what I'm trying to say, and I know what he's trying to say, and I let us both get away with it.

"Laura posted today," I say, maybe because he mentioned George. Eye for an eye. "She solved the first page."

"You must be excited."

"I am excited. But I was wondering," I say this part gently, probing, "how much could you sell me? How much do you have?"

"Just weed?"

"And Adderall?"

Matt scoffs. "That's tricky now. I did tell you." He places the joint on the edge of a glass ashtray, stands up to rifle through the box where I know he keeps his stash. I love him in this moment, all lithe, nimble fingers. He has something I want, and oh, I want.

"Four pills and as much weed as you wanna take. I can roll you some joints if you want to stay for a movie or something."

"Hmm," I say, reaching out to put the flat of my hand against his hipbone. I'm excited about the idea of getting high on Matt's stronger-than-federally-allowed weed and reading Laura's cipher. I'm excited about staying up all night applying her logic to the other encrypted pages in *The Blastments Doctrine*, scrambling for some connection. But that can wait. Yes, we could watch a movie, but I can roll my own joints. Matt puts his hand over mine and then drops to his knees in front of me. I am excited, I am excited.

Online.

It started like this: a mysterious 4chan post by a user called BlueBird claiming to be in search of highly intelligent individuals. It was a simple .jpg image, but when run through OutGuess it contained a hidden message that, unscrambled, led to an .mp3 file with reference to the Mayan calendar at specific time stamps, which combined could be turned into a URL, which led to a series of fragmented quotations from Buddhist texts, and so on. I wasn't there in those days. I was in my first year of undergrad and only just entering my decade of being chronically online. Laura was there, though, and so was Monica. I don't know how or when they met, but it must have been in the first crush of solvers. Monica had a reputation as a puzzle crafter, and Laura had a master's in math. You have never seen a talent as humble as Laura. She would post snippets of poetry and watercolour paintings of faces in other forums and then, two days later, a decryption algorithm that would propel the solving community forward with such a jolt that I would feel it in my kneecaps.

We all loved Laura, but Monica thought she loved Laura the most because they had an actual partnership. So there was Laura—a coding goddess who didn't realize she had us all enthralled—and Monica, who helped Laura with research and proofing. I'm not being unreliably competitive here. Monica was a drain on enthusiasm and a dragon guarding the castle. She was harsh on the forums where Laura was gentle and loving. She could delete posts she didn't like and shoot down newcomers for not having "been there when." You can imagine our feelings about Monica.

And then there's my friend Midi. I don't know her real name. We both became invested in the BlueBird puzzles about a year ago, but she was immediately more talented. She worshipped at the same altars, but her lines were cleaner. She made decryption look effortless, whereas I struggled until the birds starting singing morning songs outside my window. Midi was my first friend in the solving community and we had our own private server for communicating. We worked together. Our mission, like everyone else's these days, was trying to decrypt *Blastments* with its shifting codes and so, so many hidden clues. It was the last piece in BlueBird's puzzle maze.

If I'm honest, I am in the class of hobbyist codebreakers that includes hundreds, maybe thousands. I'm not special, but I thought I could be. I thought if I worked hard enough, made myself seen, I could be of service to Laura.

I really thought like this. I took my eyes off the prize of whatever was at the end of the puzzle and before I knew it had an unworthiness complex. It's not my fault. I'm in love.

Irl.

Sometimes I notice that the world is full of men. Men are statistically overrepresented in cybersecurity and cryptography, so I guess that's part of it. In general, I find them harder to talk to because they can't seem to witness the entirety of my obsession. I think really hard and fast sometimes, and this can scare people away. I look at Matt and know that I have brought this one, at least, on myself. Matt is plenty obsessive, just in different directions. He will lose himself in researching new strains of weed that don't exist in the dispensaries or in finding safe places to order pharmaceuticals online. He has a PO box connection in Norway just to get substances shipped under the radar. He can be pretty fucking obsessive. About George, for example. They were foster brothers for a few months and best friends for two decades—inseparable. But George had run for city council and won, then ran again in the next election and lost, and was now trying to figure out what to do. This process, as it turned out, involved a lot of long talks with Matt, which Matt then carried around and, occasionally, unleashed on me. I didn't really mind. Or maybe I wanted to seem like someone who didn't mind—what's the difference, really? But I guess I felt something like hot sparks inside when he said George's name or brought up city-fucking-council.

Matt was the most honest relationship I have ever had in my life because we didn't hide these things from each other. Also, he was tangible, and I wasn't getting a lot of that elsewhere. Sitting cross-legged at my desk with my eyes flitting from left to right through code hardly creates enough physical friction to be sexual, honestly, no matter how excited I get.

Sometimes I tell Matt about Laura, and he understands that I love her, and I think this is more trouble I invite upon myself. It allows him to tell me about George.

"He might go to law school," Matt says, proud.

"Gross," I say, because I can. Matt won't leave me and I won't leave him because the objects of our desire are too out of reach. I think of the puzzles when we fuck, and he closes his eyes—I think he's pretending I'm George.

Online.

We were puzzle-solvers and codebreakers staring into the void of one of the internet's most infamous mysteries. We thought of ourselves as geniuses, as critical-thinking voyagers and empresses of deductive reasoning. Uh-huh. The forums did wonders for my self-esteem and drove me out of myself. That was the problem. Without a body, I didn't always know where to go. I locked onto Laura because she was an artist, a genius, a kindness.

Laura's discovery was this: the code on the third page changed every 314 characters because the first 314 digits of π were buried in the code of the last BlueBird image, only visible if you ran the image as your operating system. Tricky stuff. Prior to this, BlueBird had coded using eight known ciphers, so Laura ran all of them with varying levels of success. Actually, it seemed that Laura had done this part together with Monica: hence the MoneyKiller shout-out. (I don't think the nickname's that clever, either.) Laura's skill was always being able to hold all of this at once. I stare at what she's done and get all teary, maybe because I know I couldn't have done this, maybe because I love her.

It turned out that BlueBird switched between only three ciphers on Laura's page: Bacon's cipher, a Null cipher, and a simple Affine cipher. Laura made this look easy, so effortless. A click of the brain, a few thousand keystrokes, and she was the premier codebreaker of a page of *Blastments*. I lit up a joint and kicked back, feeling proud of her, feeling proud of myself for knowing she existed.

What Laura decrypted was this:

I BET YOU ARE GETTING TIRED, LITTLE EYES. DO NO GIVE UP IN YOUR QUEST FOR KNOWLEDGE. KNOWLEDGE IS BURIED HERE AND WITHIN THE MANY WEBS. LIKE RAIN THAT FOLLOWS A DEATH, YOUR NEW WORLD AWAITS. LET YOUR EYES PURGE THICK AMBER AND FOLLOW THE LANGUAGE OF SPARKS AND SHRUGS. YOU AND WHAT YOU CAN ACHIEVE ARE ALL THAT MATTERS. YOUR MIND ALONE.

What Laura commented afterwards was this:

Well, I'm feeling mighty important after all that. Anyone else thinking of spiders with the whole 'webs and rain after death' thing, or is that just my phobia showing?

And oh, fuck, I loved her.

I get a message from Midi on IRC telling me to log in to Cluosh—a secure chatting program that we use to share code plus also our voices and faces. I log on immediately and Midi's talking like a bullet train to Crows, the final player in our trio. The Great Laura once shared one of Crows's algorithms and called it "genius," so he's our key to the top. He never shows his face and used to use a voice modulator but dropped that after a while. I think he has a crush on Midi, and she thinks he has a crush on me, so we both play a little silly around him, sometimes, as a wink to each other.

"Hey Kye," Crows says. "How are you doing today?" Crows is from Austria and speaks English well, if a little formally.

"Eh. Still working customer support for a scam. You know."

"I thought UltraTax was real," he says.

"Dude. You should see the way they trick you into paying. It's a maze," Midi supplies. "Just another puzzle."

"Not the fun kind," I say. They're going to fire me soon, I can feel it, but I don't say this because we have bigger fish to fry. "You read it?"

"Fuck off," Midi says. "I can't believe we missed π."

"I blame Crows," I say. "You know math."

"I'm fucking shit at stego and you know it," Crows bites. English might be his second language, but cussing comes easy.

"She's a genius," Midi sighs. "Monica must be so high on herself right now."

"I don't want to think about it." I myself am still high on weed and awe and don't want to be pulled back down just yet. "Drawing on all those ciphers," I say, "is just so pretty, isn't it?"

“Yeah, yeah,” Crows says. He loves Laura, too, but pretends weariness at our fawning. I think he likes to remind us that Laura has acknowledged his existence by acting casual about her. “The important thing is that we have, ah, very many leads.”

“Cipher-switching. Ciphers inside ciphers inside ciphers. It’s too much,” Midi says, but her tone is excited. It’s a lot, almost infinite, maybe actually infinite, but it’s something. And it’s open, now. Anyone could have the idea, could find another hidden message. Anyone could be the next Laura. We’re all thinking it.

“Let’s make a task list,” I say. “Let’s send this thing. I hope you guys didn’t have weekend plans.”

Irl.

Matt told me that I could come over at four but that I should text him before I leave in case he’s asleep. I text at 3:30 and hear nothing, again at 3:45, but still nothing. I decide to leave the house at four anyway. It’s spitting rain, but not so bad. My hair might frizz up, but Matt’s seen it worse, obviously.

I like being outside when it’s like this. It’s December now—eight days since Laura posted the new page of *Blastments*—but not cold. A crisp two degrees and grey. I have been inside in furnaced conditions for long enough that every part of me feels dehydrated. I imagine myself soaking up the drizzle like lotion, as if I were a desert lizard with permeable skin. Can you imagine that kind of vulnerability? I shake a little and walk faster to warm up.

I’m walking towards Matt’s apartment, but in a meandering kind of way in case he doesn’t get back to me or changes his mind. Plus, if he did text back and tell me he was up, I wouldn’t want to be too close and seem like I was waiting outside his door or something. I dip into a used bookstore just to get out of the wet for a few moments. I always go to the weird little back sections. Used bookstores are often cramped and there's always someone with a backpack pushing through, knocking you into things. The back corner is safe, and this also happens to be, most often, where the castoff books are. I once found a back-corner book called *Lobsters: Gangsters of the Sea* by Mary M. Cerullo. I still have it facing outwards on my bookshelf in the hopes that someone will ask me about it. Today I can see a hardboiled detective paperback called *The Old Dick* and feel compelled to get it for Matt as a belated birthday gift, but then the man himself texts me "anytime" and I feel so irritated by this single-word reply that I decide he doesn't deserve the book.

I poke around the bookstore for a little while longer and pick up a two-dollar edition of *Hamlet* with a cool skull illustration on the front. Then I make my way back out into the rain and towards Matt.

He's acting weird when I get there. He's pacing and offers me the joint in his hand before I even take off my damp jacket. I decline and notice the pile of roaches in the ash tray. I ask him how he's doing and put a little emphasis on it so that he knows I'm not being casual.

"Well," he says, and I brace myself, I really do. "George thinks I'm being cruel."

"You do a lot for him," I exhale, taking off my jacket and hanging it on a hook. I drop my bag on the ground and go to sit on his couch. You can't see much out his windows because of the fog. I couldn't live in a high-rise, but I do love being in them. "What cruelty could you have managed?"

"Not to him," he says. "To, uh, you?"

"George thinks—wait, hold on." I have to collect myself here. I stop looking out the window and look right at him. I can feel a teeny-tiny fire inside me that could easily turn into tears or rage. Either would be disastrous. "George doesn't get an opinion on me," I say. I want him to know I feel invaded. I want him to hurt, too.

"Well," Matt says, and he rubs the back of his neck, then jumps as an ember from his joint falls and burns through his sock. Good.

"You're not cruel to me," I say firmly because I can see where this is going and I won't go gently.

"You have feelings." He is not looking at me because he has made up his mind. I can see it now. I wonder if he was even sleeping before. Maybe he was talking to *him*. Maybe he was here, sitting where I am sitting, talking about me while I looked at *The Old Dick*. I feel sick. I start to deny the feelings, but I can feel my throat get sticky with the pre-crying routine and I hate it, I hate it, I hate it.

"Fuck," I say, then push my fingers into my hairline. I am mad at myself for walking around in the rain because now my hair does not look its best, and my makeup is probably all clumpy, and everything is very bad.

"I have like twelve Adderalls," he says. "I'll give you all of them when you go."

"Okay," I say, because—tell me—what the fuck else am I supposed to do?

*

When I get home, I see an email from my supervisor at UltraTax informing me I've been laid off. They don't go into reasons, but I am finding that reasons tend only to make things worse these days.

Online.

Should I talk about Sisyphus here? That's what they always say about BlueBird—the journalists and the bloggers outside the solving community. "Sisyphean." I wish I had known that term before I chose my screen name, which actually comes from my favourite Sylvia Plath poem because I made the damn thing when I was fourteen years old. *IsolateSlowFaults*. Don't blame me for my melodrama. I felt incapable of more knowledge, as Sylvia would say. Little did either of us know.

Now that I have no day job and no drug-dealer-with-benefits to worry about, I can dedicate all my time to cribbing and steganography. I keep careful records of everything I try and everything that Midi and Crows try, too. I am putting more hours in than either of them, which is why it's annoying when Midi finds something real.

Midi works in some kind of office where she can't do deep-dive work during the day, but she can trawl through message boards and read other people's suggestions if her boss isn't around. Someone mentioned the fact that rain and death had been heavily cited together last summer, when one of the effects of climate change was new flooding in a Chilean desert that killed a bunch of microbiomes. There was precedent for BlueBird to talk of a climate apocalypse, which lined up nicely with the strangely cryptic, urgent tone of the page. The coordinates of the desert were cited online as 23.8634° S, 69.1328° W, which could be run through cipher algorithms the same way that Laura had used π. Midi had tried a little on her own and saw some patterns, so she brought what she had to Crows and me.

I didn't hold my breath—I gasped great lungfuls of air as I ran Bacon and Null and Vigenère and even, with a little finagling, Stream ciphers. And yeah, there was something here, all right.

*

We have enough to share, and the three of us decide that Midi should be the one to post what we have uncovered in the forum. Midi had, after all, been the one to find the coordinates. I know it's the right thing to do even though this is the most jealous I have ever been in my life. I am a good person, and I suppress the urge to send Matt a message explaining the situation so that he can compliment my restraint. I impose cruelty upon myself, thank you very much.

Our little trio is together on Cluosh when Monica direct messages Midi. Midi squeals a little and reads out the message.

"Nice work with this. I would love to talk further. Let me know when you're free?"

"Can you believe? This is, like, actual validation in the community."

"She's such a gatekeeper," I say. "'Nice work with this'? Who cares what she thinks."

"You do. I do. Laura does."

"Eh," says Crows. "Call me when you get past MoneyKiller."

"I'm telling her that I'm free whenever. I can call in sick tomorrow if she can't talk tonight," Midi says, and I feel jealous of her lax employment situation in the face of my lack of one. We continue to run variations of ciphers through the text and make slow progress. We've got a couple of English words sorted: *most weak hams.* Too strange to make any sense, but too coincidentally

English to be a mistake. I'm half asleep at my desk, listening to our shared SoundCloud playlist and the unmuted clicks of Crows' typing when Midi chirps back to life. "Tomorrow morning," she says. "Monica wants to chat tomorrow morning."

*

I turn off my alarm with the intention of getting up, but fall back asleep. I wake again at 11 a.m. to a screenful of unread messages from Midi and—*fuck*—one from Matt.

I click that one first, obviously.

—*Hey Kye. I feel a bit bad about everything. Like, I shouldn't have dropped that on you without warning. And I think I made it sound like George didn't like you, and it's not like that at all. Anyways, if you want to get a beer or something, let me know.*

Oh, fuck him. I open the first message from Midi and read through.

—*Where are you?*

—*Kye. Kye!*

—*When you wake up you're gonna be so mad you missed this and I want to tell you over Cluosh, bitch.*

—*Ok. FINE. So.*

—*Monica said she played around with it and didn't think it was anything. She told me to delete the post from the forum so people don't waste their time.*

—*!!!*

—*Wake the fuck up. I'm so mad right now and I'm going to take it out on you if you don't get the fuck online.*

The last message was sent fifteen minutes ago, so I log on all sleepy-haired and blurry and scratch at my eyebrow as the internet catches up on what sounds like a parrot being electrocuted. Everything buffers and I realize that Midi is shouting. All-caps lock. She looks worse than I do.

"KYE."

"I saw your messages."

"FUCK."

"Why is she doing this?"

"Ummmm. Because she wants to take my idea and show it to Laura herself, obviously."

"Hams is pigs, right?" Crows says, and honestly, I didn't realize he was online.

"Fuck her!" Midi says. "I'm not deleting the post."

"They will bury it," Crows says with a tiredness that makes me think he's already said this. "Monica can have it reported and removed."

"You could message Laura," I say, stupidly. I haven't woken up yet. Midi doesn't even dignify me with a response.

"We don't need her support," Midi says. "We can crack this on our own, you know. We don't need any of them."

"We could..." says Crows. He'd be the one building the algorithms, for the most part, and he knows it. We've been at this for days, and we have three words that we're not even a hundred percent sure of. Besides, without Laura, without anyone even seeing what we've done, the impetus melts away. I've long ago come to terms with the fact that I am in this for my idols. For Laura. She doesn't check her messages, inundated as she is by hundreds of solvers every day with this or that trite suggestion. Everything—and I mean everything—goes through Monica.

"MoneyKiller probably won't go to Laura with just the pigs," Crows says. He means the hams. He's hooked on the hams. "She'll need more."

"But we're stuck," I say. "They could be using a new cipher—one we haven't thought of yet."

"She doesn't know what we've tried," Crows says. "No such thing as useless information. We could keep working, as we have been."

"If we get more than 'weak hams' we could put a real argument forward," I say. "Maybe get other people to back us. Maybe a critical mass?"

"Monica would only acknowledge a lot of people," Crows says. "We could break this open."

"Fine," Midi says. "Fine. I took a sick day anyways. Let's de-needle this hay farm, I guess."

Irl.

How frustrating to be a carbon-based body in need of maintenance. I go to the corner store just before they close at 7 p.m., hoping that no one will notice my sweatsuit and greasy hair and bleary, screen-burnt eyes in the December darkness. I buy instant noodles and a KitKat bar with coins. I have maybe two months of savings before a job becomes necessary again. How secondly frustrating to be a genius under capitalism. I am frustration, personified. My knees ache and my feet do not like to hold my weight up. I haven't moved much in three days. The only sense I remember is sight, because lord knows I haven't considered taste or smell or sound or the other one lately. Right, touch. I certainly haven't considered touch in a while.

When I get back to my house there's a person on my porch. I jump a little, still nervous about being seen by someone who doesn't have the customer-service skill of object impermanence. I recognize the shape of his head and this instantly irritates me.

"What?" I say. He starts to talk but I cut him off. "I was gone for two minutes and somehow you're here? On my porch? What the fuck?"

"I was across the street," Matt says. "On the bench." He gestures to the church across from my house. "I saw you leave."

"Stalker."

He smiles, small. "Guess so."

We stand there for a moment and I get even angrier because it's obviously not my turn to talk. I just want to go into my house. I'm cold and I shiver dramatically to show him.

"Can I come in?"

"No." I stare at him and he just keeps smiling at me in a way I haven't seen before. "Fine. Shove over." I unlock my door with as much distance from his body as I can manage. When I get inside, I flick on the lights that haven't been used in a few days. I mostly stay in my bedroom with my computer.

"Are you okay?" he asks.

"Are *you* okay?" I snap. "You're in my house. What do you want?"

"You didn't text me back."

"You broke up with me."

"I wanted to talk to you."

"Did you bring drugs?"

"No. Well, yeah, actually, but look—"

"What do you want from me?" I say. I want to make my soup and get back to my laptop. I was onto something before my stomach forced me into the real world. I can't remember what it was right now, but it was itchy and good.

"I guess a few things," he says. "I wanted to apologize, and—and I wanted to make sure you were okay. I wanted to see if you wanted to, I don't know, try again?"

"I guess a few things," I mirror. "No to your apology. I am perfectly fine, thank you, and, um, fuck you."

"Okay. You—Kye. You don't seem fine."

"Get out," I say, and I mean for it to come out authoritative, but I kind of break with tiredness on the second word.

"You're decrypting," he says. "Did you figure something out? Are you working with her?" The way he says *her* makes me realize something. We have jealousy in common, Matt and I. I choose violence.

"Yeah. And she says you're too cruel to me. So get out."

He goes back to the door, and I immediately realize that this is not the note that I want to end on. I liked the way the last song ended: me shuffling out of his foggy high-rise with a pocketful of stimulants. This is the opposite of that. I feel pathetic and sad. He coughs into his fist and says, "You should, I don't know, eat a vegetable."

"I lost my job," I say, because now I don't want him to leave. I can't get him to stay with charm and allure, not tonight, so I go full pathetic. It's a risk, but I'm out of moves. "And, yeah, we found a pattern. It's tricky. It's taking a lot out of me. And I—there's no one home, by the way. Roommates are gone for the holidays." International code, that. He pauses and considers, perhaps weighing ethics and consequences and horniness against each other. Ethics are ants next to the elephant of horniness, so I know that I've won. He asks if I want to watch a movie and I ask if he wants to share his drugs.

*

Matt always sleeps longer and heavier than I do. I peel myself from the bed and try to boot up my computer, but it's dead. This is why you can't trust men. They distract and they take and all of a sudden you forget basic needs, like battery life. Speaking of basic needs, I go to the bathroom and start up the shower for the first time in a week. I swear to god, it sputters from disuse. I should be ashamed, but I'm a little proud. After the shower, I put on a nice sweater and actual jeans and climb back into bed next to Matt. He's still out, so I pick up the copy of *Hamlet* that I got at the used bookstore and start flipping through it.

I loved this play in high school. The only Shakespeare I liked, and I liked it because I love madness, and I love fake madness, and I loved that Laertes was sketchily obsessed with his hot sister. I wrote an essay about that and got 65 percent because people are afraid of the truth if it's not right in front of their eyes. Obsession is the only truth and it's in everything, it's everywhere.

Here is Hamlet roasting Polonius, a silly old perv if ever there was one, and here is the part where—where—

I read it three times and I can't breathe. I can't—

I go to my computer and log onto everything as fast as I can. I've password-protected the shit out of this whole thing, so it takes a while, plus I keep making typos because my fingers are getting ahead of themselves. Then I'm in, and I'm holding the book up with one hand and typing the passage in with two fingers. I send:

> HAMLET. *For the satirical rogue says here that old men have gray beards, that their faces are wrinkled, their eyes purging thick amber and plum-tree gum, and that they have a plentiful lack of wit, together with most weak hams—all which, sir, though I most powerfully and potently believe, yet*

I hold it not honesty to have it thus set down; for yourself, sir, should be old as I am, if like a crab you could go backward.

And then I wait.

Online.

It's enough. If every page has an allusion to *Hamlet*, that gives us enough restrictions to work with. There is no infinity here, and nothing has ever felt more freeing. *Hamlet* might be Shakespeare's longest play, but it's still only about thirty thousand words long.

Pretty quickly, we start to find patterns. The "eyes purging thick amber" bit was mentioned in Laura's page and comes from the same speech in act 2, scene 2. More follows from there and we realize that the number two is a key. After a few diligent days (me) and evenings (Midi and Crows), we have pages. Three of them, to be exact. One for each of us. Crows says: no man left behind. We have to decide what we're going to do next. The original plan was to decrypt enough so that the community couldn't ignore us, but that was when we were seeking words, phrases. We never expected pages.

We spend a fair amount of time lamenting our lack of access to Laura, direct. We consider Crows and his standing with her, but he humbly—and for the first time—admits that one shout-out doth not a friend make. We talk in circles. We forget to eat. We get giddy with our achievement and then remember that it's for nothing if it does not lead us somewhere.

People like us solve puzzles to prove something.

Our choice ends up being made for us when Laura updates the forum with a post.

*Update: ***New pattern found*** [LauraLies & MoneyKiller] Ah! Something new, from our own MoneyKiller—Monica did it again with her crushable cribbing skills. We love her, we do. Go forth and use these coordinates and see if you can find anything else. Mwah.*

After that, we were pretty set on evading the influence of Monica.

*

We start by reaching out to individual solvers who we feel are on our level. It's a hierarchical thing, I know, but it's a hierarchical world, and if anyone wants to suggest a realistic way to dismantle it, I'm all ears. You have to understand how many laypeople exist here. Say BlueBird at a party and I guarantee someone will have heard about it.

We work to increase our impact among our peers, but it feels like we're giving away something precious. I know it's the right thing to do, but I almost instantly mourn the days when I was one of three people who had the key, when I was keeper of the code.

I distract myself with what I plan on doing when I get Laura's attention. I imagine it playing out like this: Laura will praise us our ingenuity, will specifically note the *Hamlet* connection as astute and brilliant. Maybe I will say something wise about literature, something that lights her up. I compliment her style—the sharpness of her coding and steadfast dedication to BlueBird (and throw in a line or two about her watercolour prowess), and then we start a private server just to talk about puzzles and art and how we love to feel connected to something bigger than us. Then she tells me what city she lives in and I move there and we live together and are in love forever.

Or maybe we just become friends who follow each other on social media—like all the normal non-paranoids around us. I would settle for her Instagram handle, I really would.

Most likely she compliments everyone's hard work and we all move on. *The Blastments Doctrine* is solved, and our community dissolves before our eyes, leaving us with strange skills and memories. Whoever BlueBird is reaches out, congratulates us, gives the smartest among us jobs with the CIA or a think-tank, or maybe there's a prize. I don't care. I don't spend a lot of time on this. I visualize becoming a helium balloon let loose when this is over, drifting into the big blue and understanding my inevitable death. Maybe I will spend a week without Wi-Fi. Maybe I will go on a blind date with a stranger. Oh, god. I turn my focus back to sharing my secrets and spreading Shakespeare's Good Word. I will not live normally, I know.

Irl.

Matt is sitting across from me at Future Bistro. It's bottomless pierogi night. I am staring into a stout. Matt ordered the eggnog cocktail and makes a wincing face every time he sips. I told him not to get it, but he can be an idiot when it comes to listening to me. Neither of us have pierogis but all the undergrad kids around us do and the whole place smells like onions. I do love this city, but it's complicated. I love Matt, too, but it's also complicated. Right now he is breaking up with me again, but I am not upset about it because I am also breaking up with him. You know when people say their breakup was mutual and you understand that they're lying? Well, I'm also lying, but I am not going to say in which direction. Live with it.

He tells me about how George has decided to become a lawyer and I say that I already knew that and he says that, no, George was just thinking about it back then. Whatever. It has been three weeks since Laura acknowledged our work on BlueBird. I was pretty fucked up about it for a bit because that's what an anticlimax does to someone with my obsessive nature. She acknowledged us as a collective and stated her intention to wait to hear anything from the mysterious BlueBird. In my sadness, I tried to break up with Matt, but he wouldn't let me. He just kept showing up at my house with mandarin oranges and talking about scurvy. We are both healthy enough to break up tonight, on pierogi night, so that's what we are doing. I tell him that I got over BlueBird; I moved on. He points out a "Now Hiring" sign near the register. We smile at each other. We joke about that time he stalked me. I think we'll stay friends, but who knows. I'll cry if I think that the last time I was in his apartment was the final time I would look out through the foggy clouds at the purple-blue-green haze of the CN Tower, so I don't think about it.

Midi gave me her Instagram handle. Her name is Jennifer and she mostly posts pictures of skylines at night. We comment on each other's posts and stories and one day I might go to Seattle to visit her. Crows would lose his mind—he might even show us his face on Cluosh if we make him jealous enough.

Matt pushes his eggnog at me and says, with gravity, "Try it."

"You wish."

"Try it or I'll break up with you," he says, loud enough for the table of undergrads behind us to pause their conversation. He doesn't smile and neither do I; we commit to the bit.

"You'd break up with me because of my egg allergy?" I accuse loudly.

"It's not just the eggs and you know it. The dairy! The gluten! I just can't live with your dietary restrictions anymore!"

"I hope you die of scurvy!"

"I hope you die of dysentery!" He can't do it anymore and laughs, and I laugh too. And whatever I deserve, I don't know, but I feel lucky to have what I have, and I feel lucky to be in a body again. I look around the restaurant in search of a screen and find a TV playing the news, always the news, even here.

Alex Leslie

THE FORMULA

I've known Costa for more than ten years now and I remember the moment we met, they opened the door at the youth detox the day after I was hired, their eyes wide, their hair tangled, it's one of the two times I've looked at someone and known *we are going to know each other for a long time* and what do you do with a feeling like that except grip it close, knowing I'll never really be ever rid of you, we are never going to not know each other? Friendship was the only religion that made sense to me after I left home, *left* is a euphemism, my mom sat on the taped-up leather couch in her sunroom cluttered with laundry detergent boxes and wilted rubber trees draped in Christmas lights and said *I'll never accept you I'm proud of my traditional upbringing*, it's that kind of moment that ends one life and starts another, things like that made me into this kind of person, a queer who sees another queer in a doorway and thinks *we are going to know each other for a long time*, that's how I met Costa.

The first thing I really loved about Costa was their laugh, how their laughter starts out loud, then retreats like a flashy animal burrowing down their skinny throat into a pink-tented home, finishes with Costa twisting their chin, the animal's tail vanishing between their chipped teeth, they laughed at my shyness, laughed at falling objects. No one else laughed like that, from thunder to murmur, everybody else laughed the reverse, small to big, I did too, and Costa had no idea how unlikely their laugh was, I loved to hear it. We watched reality TV surrounded by teenagers oozing drugs from their pores, the detox was in a rundown duplex by the river's oily sleep, Costa had worked there for years and watched the drugs get deadly, our job was to be support workers which meant we were lifeguards at the pool of opiate withdrawal, we chatted with nurses who rotated with Dixie Cups of blue pills big as plum pits, we answered phones and poured Kool-Aid, truth serum in pink streams. The teenagers stayed for a few days, drowsy in their rooms, curled up between us, returned again and again, they came with backpacks full of muddy shirts, we wore thick garden gloves to sort the laundry in case of syringes, in the beginning I heard nurses complain that the sickest ones were "frequent flyers," said *they just use this place like a homeless shelter*, Costa never said that stuff, Costa folded their shirts like letters to friends, I thought I'd do the job for a few months for some cash but I stayed two years, because Costa.

Costa's eyes are so still and blue they can ask any question and it feels like a compliment, I watched them draw kids out so smooth, so slow, the kids at the detox all loved Costa's laugh and how it cascaded and fled, I wanted to be filled with that sea lion bark, I used to think Costa found everything funny on some level, now I know different. On those couches, I told Costa the whole story of my life, they were the first person I'd told the whole story to front to back, I told my life like a spine-split novel, about my dad's houseboat that caught fire, about a road trip to Whitehorse to hook up with an older paleontologist who stole my wallet, I was so lonely in those days, out of touch with my family and working nights with Costa and doing grade twelve math and geography on the library computers to be able to apply to college, the job of waiting out dopesickness made it easy to ramble to Costa, an unquenchable bleed of sound came from me, we weren't going to quit because we were both getting paid to *do human*, that's what we called it.

It was the always-situation with my brother that I was venting about when Costa told me about the Formula, their skinny legs knotted around a pillow like a birthing exercise, I told them about my big brother and why we didn't talk anymore, it was in that zone between 1 and 4 a.m. and the whole thing came out about how my brother kicked me out of his place after my mom kicked me out, that was four years ago and now we didn't talk, he texted long whinges about his job managing Boston Pizzas, *but then where did you go*, said Costa. Here's the thing about Ike, I told Costa, all the light off the TV's huge moon cheek swarming in their eyes, my brother Ike is a cruel person but thinks he is a practical person and no matter what he does he'll argue he did the logical thing, he put my stuff on the sidewalk in plastic bins and texted me *I'm just trying to help you keep momentum*, that's the worst part, knowing it was pragmatic to him, I had nowhere, back in those days I couldn't stop obsessing over whether my mom had told my brother to kick me out or if he'd done it on his own, Costa was the only person I unspooled this to, and they never told me their story back.

Costa's hair was freshly violet, I remember because their skin was scorched tulip petals at the hairline, they reached out and rubbed the untouched spot between my thumb and index finger, they said *don't give him any more of your words he eats them just like cereal in milk.* Like the instant they opened the door and I saw Costa for the first time, I knew this moment was a fishing lure sunk in my memory's ribcage, down, down, *words just like cereal in milk*, it's still what appears in my mind when I'm talking with someone at a committee meeting who can't listen, a picture of sentences slopping from a milky spoon into their greedy mouth, *cereal in milk.* Listen, Costa said, listen, I'll tell you my Formula for texting with people who fuck with my head, I send back three random emojis, just random enough, I let the list of emojis scroll by and send three really random ones, it just works, people make a story out of whatever you send, it's a way to send a something-nothing, it's magic. They whispered it, that last part, *something-nothing, magic*, and I knew they were telling me something private and true, the world *magic* mouse-trapped in my chest, a recognition of how Costa's disappointment in people was so pure it was distilled and sinister, a tiny bottle they set in my palm, the Formula.

That was years ago and I can't count the number of times I've used the Formula since then, it's part of my arsenal now, how I do people, every time I use it I feel Costa rubbing the softest part of my hand during my story of exile, the instructions about the Formula, the cool pleasure that soared in me at Costa's touch, and a fear, thinking *if you can cut people off that easily you can cut me off.* Ike was the first person I used the Formula on, he texted me how our mom won her war over the neighbour's hedge by pouring rat poison into the roots and the neighbour's thirteen-year-old labradoodle died by accident, our mom who wasn't in touch with me but my brother acted like she was, I swiped the menu of emojis at the bottom of my screen and my thumb touched down, once, twice, three times. Since my brother kicked me out because my mom told him to, or because he was just an asshole, I'd demoted him to newsletter status, the *keeping busy*s, the *holding up*s, the *lots on my plate*s, but now I followed Costa's Formula and sent the three emojis, a chef holding a spoon, a crow, and a blue heart.

My brother's name filled my screen, IKE MOSS, the first time he'd tried to phone me since the inception of our silence, and I pressed the red circle, *you working in a restaurant now?* he texted, *hey pick up, everything okay?*, the crow and the blue heart shimmered ominously beside the chef, who exuded chipper confidence and gripped his spoon like a wizard's magic staff, and my brother texted a teeming block of question marks. I was lying in the grit of my sheets I washed when a hook-up was coming over to fuck, infrequent enough for my sheets to feel like an arid beach, and I imagined my brother's mottled hazel eyes decrypting the chef and crow and heart, I felt my breath slip out of my chest, I texted Costa, *it works*, their response instantaneous, *magic*, and a few seconds later, they sent me an emoji of a cup of coffee, a dancing robot, and an emoji hugging itself, then a selfie, Costa shirtless, fat pink lips, blue eyes, hair swept over in a flawless green wave, shoulders glowing slim and bright, backlit hills in the slushy field of flash on pillow.

I got into college, quit the detox and I knew Costa was wounded when I left but I said nothing to them, I just couldn't take watching the kids sweat and puke anymore and hearing how many died from overdoses, I told myself I was starting over, my little list of computer language courses like a precious one-way train ticket, and when we texted they never asked about school, just updates about our nurse-nemesis Kailey and our favourite detox kids in choppy lines, and our friendship shifted into long phone calls when they were working nights at the detox, I talked about how I never heard from my mom but I was trying not to care and I talked about my one girlfriend who broke up with me during a programming lecture and Costa told me vignettes about everyone who lived in their little apartment building, the woman who skipped rope on their ceiling, there were long silences on those calls, we sat together breathing, I could hear the detox TV in the background, and Costa's mouth-wind like my own personal static. When I didn't hear back from them for three weeks after my exams I texted ghost ghost ghost, biked through the hot May rain, the season's newly opened hands rubbing my cheeks. On the second floor of the detox Costa was on the couch, neck folded, osmosing a fourteen-year-old's story about being given a pass to a gym, swanky, fluorescent lights, house music, the kid hadn't known what the gym pass meant, but he loved having the longest showers ever and he slept on the green velvet couch in the locker room and when the dealer who gave him the pass asked him to beat someone up he just did it, and now that he was coming off all the down he saw all the faces, the noses buckling, the knuckles hosing, the whole broken-head movie, I lived through the zombie apocalypse, he told Costa, sobs cresting, Costa reached for his hand, said, I did too.

Costa's hair was bleached and past their chin, their face narrowed, eyes lively as water sliding around smooth rocks, we stood in the kitchen and Costa rolled up cheese slices and devoured them like a snake absorbing a bird, they told me they'd been *up and down, my usual low-key rollercoaster, you know*, I asked if they were okay and they said, *tell me everyone who you've used the Formula on, it'll make me happy.* I told them how the Formula had helped me with Ike, he'd stopped sending the rants and now, every Sunday, sent three emojis, always pretty ones, sparrow tulip angel, cupcake mouse Christmas tree, and I responded with as much truthfulness as I could muster about how I felt towards him and our mom, peace-sign alien planet, snowman rainbow popcorn, my thumb alighting mindless, selecting my symbols for me, like Costa said, and that was how my brother and I sent little fires between our screens, here I am, ocean lightbulb boy. Milk lightbulb skeleton, Costa smiled listening, I told them that my mom texted me for the first time since she'd thrown me out, since that final sunroom conversation, *Ike tells me you're doing well, nice to hear you're back in school and on good terms with your brother, Love Your Mum*, and my thumb alighted on house cloud turtle, pictures that made my stomach seep lemon water, an hour later she texted back, *you're very busy with school I understand it is nice to hear from you*, as if I'd been the one who had ruined my own life, and Costa nodded and exhaled, *mazel tov*, their ironic laugh jumped, Costa's irises shimmering tidal pool clear, I dipped my fingertips right into their pupils, right down into their ink, and I said, *how long?*

We spent the next week on the couch, my housemates were away for Christmas, and Costa bucked in the couch's soft ditch, I DoorDashed Kool-Aid, stirred it with a little warm water like I'd seen the nurses do for nausea, and tipped it down Costa's throat, they asked me to put on *Good Will Hunting*, a movie they'd seen a million times that calmed them down, and then they asked me to lie on top of them to weigh down their shaking, a quilt and a blanket between our bodies, Robin Williams's voice droned on about friends and war, and Costa slept, when I got up

I looked back down at them and dragged a layer of sweat off their forehead with the coast of my hand, and I put my hand to my own forehead and felt all of their cold and heat together, I wanted to kiss their eyelids, those familiar suns. I'd been protected from the heroin withdrawals at the detox, kids kept to their rooms for the worst of it, but with Costa I felt it all, they said me weighing them down got rid of the bone hurt, I felt their marrow cook, I felt their breath separate from their brain with a low ripping sound, I kept rice steaming into a porridge with brown sugar and ginger, something I remembered my mom did once when I had teeth pulled, hot spoon like a second tongue, her voice, her dressing gown filling a doorway.

We talked about the Formula, Costa told me how they discovered it, it was when they changed their name, their mom said the same thing to them that my mom said to me about being gay, *I'll never accept you I'm proud of my traditional upbringing*, like they'd both trained from the same shitty-mom handbook, and when Costa moved out here to be close to the ocean and become Costa, their mom sent long texts as if nothing had happened, one night Costa's thumb punched out a big block of emojis and they selected three, it was chicken raindrop traffic-light, and they sent it and laughter shook their body, their body was like that instrument that plays through the air, you know the one, theremin, yeah, theremin, they'd never laughed like that before, a laugh like a spinal fluid spasm, they threw up on the kitchen floor, strange water. It felt so good that Costa kept using the Formula, for the ex they lived with in a van for six months after their last homeless shelter, she turned vicious in close quarters, their text exchange was just her rage paragraphs then Costa's emoji trios in between, Costa said, *everyone told me to block her but being silent and weird is much more powerful, I used the Formula for dealers too, I used it for my sister, I used it for landlords, I never block anyone, I hate that, blocking is weakness*, and I let Costa mutter this all out, it was the sixth day in my apartment together, a day of black coffee, frozen pizza, and quiet litanies.

The next part is what I've never told to my fiancée, Lu, friends or anyone, the last day on the couch we spent naked, I swear it was Costa who started things, I felt the blanket coming out from between our bodies, when Costa's fingers felt under the elastic of my boxers I scurried out of them so fast, I pressed my shoulder into the hollow beside Costa's neck and my fingers plunged inside them with such pure knowing of what I wanted, as I pulled my fingers out of them, their face strobed in my mind, like their face the moment we met, when they opened the door of the detox, do you know your moments of inevitability embedded in days and doors, Costa smelled like a week of cheese and Kool-Aid, they were slick with the drug cold-pressed from their pores, fully juiced, skinnier than I'd fantasized, sketch and hinge under their sweatpants and binder. When I woke, Costa was gone, I lay on the couch until the nest of young birds in my stomach snarled upward at my mind, I piled seven pizza boxes on top of the sink, I drained the last of the colour from the pitcher, I walked to my regular coffee shop, the rain battered my hood in a way I'd never known rain before, pellets rang hard off my small moving tent, each drop a discrete bullet, I drank sour espresso at the window, my fingers, the bank of morning steam, the cup, it all smelled like Costa, I sat until my phone buzzed, shooting-star turtle skull, and I did not hear from Costa again after that for two years.

Costa said a thing to me when we worked at the detox, *you don't talk like anyone else I know, you talk the way a hummingbird drinks from a feeder, you don't finish thoughts you just kind of hover around and sip and keep going.* The hummingbird accusation repeated on the loop-track that runs at a diagonal around my skull, the tilted ring of a planet, a groove in the bone that hosts the worst thoughts that orbit me, some stay for days, some for years, never truly leaving but continuing a quick song along the ridges, until summoned, it haunted me, *you never finish thoughts*, I told my boring friends at my lab job the hummingbird thing and everyone agreed that Costa sounded sketchy, what kind of person takes off like that after the way I helped them, but I left out part of the story, as in the part that I was in love with Costa, I couldn't close the space they had opened inside me so instead I raged about the hummingbird comment, how dare they know my hovering.

My fiancée, Lu, when I met her on the third day of my next job, I recognized the always-already feeling from Costa, this time I played it smart, on our fourth date I informed Lu about the feeling, *I know we are going to know each other for a very long time*, and she smiled, moved forward, removed the bandanna from her hair, and unzipped my pants in a single gesture. After our first big fight I used the Formula on her, tugboat avocado dinosaur, and she texted back WTF?????????????? and turned up at my place, my housemate pretending to scramble eggs while I feebly explained the Formula, as soon as it left my lips I understood it was a mistake to speak it to Lu, a bigger mistake to blame in on Costa, revealed how we spoke with each other. *What kind of a person comes up with something like that*, Lu said, whirling her arms, and I watched my housemate laugh so hard that eggs fell out of his mouth, there was no explaining Costa, no defending Costa, Costa was Costa, I told Lu, I couldn't explain it, like I couldn't explain why when my mom died a year later the first person I needed to tell was Costa, we hadn't spoken since we'd had sex, I was on the toilet at work crying from head to toe and I texted: gravestone gravestone waving-hand mom.

Three months four days clean was the first thing Costa said to me the next day when I took the SkyTrain and a bus to their place out in the suburbs, a bungalow with a yard for their stripey Rottweilerish mutt, they sat cross-legged on their couch, they asked questions about my mother, not about how she died but about who she'd been, I talked about her framed oil paintings of women with braids, how the painted braids seemed to me like poised snakes, the rubber trees she draped with Christmas lights, the line of sand in the bathroom sink because she rinsed her watershoes there after her morning swim in the ocean, those swims were the only thing that kept her mood stable, her revolting soups, fruit cocktail and chicken and dumplings, chili with Cool Ranch Doritos, her jars of sun tea on top of the fridge that she called *dry-drunk moonshine*, her wet footprints on the hall's scratched-down carpets that cured into salt stains, Ike moved back in there for the final months of her life, never told me she was sick, he packed photographs, her Bible and her watershoes into a box and sent them to me, he emailed me a photo of her beloved sunroom in its final incarnation, a black leather couch framed by rubber trees and piles of newspapers, *oh you grew up in the detox that's why you loved working there so much*, Costa said, and they laughed, just like the hummingbird comment this hit me quiet, their beard piled big and soft on their chest, the way they touched their beard I could tell they were pleased by its heft, their laugh was still a whole self-contained language for me, many words spoken at once, a full-circle uttering, and they got up from the couch to pour the coffee that was placed steeping on the radiator, white gills breathing warm air on Costa's bright shadow.

There was a river close by where we walked their mutt in mucky halfmoon beaches among the toothy rocks, we watched barges stacked with cars glimmer by, *spaceships*, Costa murmured, I waited for Costa to apologize for what had happened between us, I'd fantasized that Costa would turn to me and say *I recognize now how I mishandled things, I value our friendship*, but nothing came, so I told them the story of trying to use the Formula on Lu, they laughed so hard the dog came running up and pummelled their chest, crying with worry. I asked Costa if they still used the Formula and they nodded to the rhythm of their dipping joint, *oh yeah sometimes, yeah the only person I use it with the most is my sister*, a wave at a tugboat, *your sister?*, I said cautiously and Costa nodded, told me how their sister sent them photos of her garden, nephews' birthday cakes, *your basic milestone shit*, still used Costa's deadname, Auntie. They told me about their job managing inventory at a pharmacy, their weight-lifting routine, the guy they were dating, *don't worry I didn't meet him in a recovery group*, Ned, an introvert who owned three trucks and taught music to seniors, they didn't ask me if there would be a funeral, they didn't ask about Lu or when our wedding would be, they pointed at the cars on barges, chanted in their new, deep, gorgeous voice, *Subaru Toyota Subaru.*

After that, Costa was in and out of our apartment every few weeks for dinners for a couple years, Lu surprised me with her immediate, total fondness for Costa, she went on and on about Costa's talent for pacing the humour in a story precisely right, how they always came to dinners with a homemade cake, their back-pounding hugs, she said *I'm so glad you have someone you can open up to since you lost your brother*, she adored their big dog named Uber Alice, and I saw how Costa had fooled her, like they fooled people, I watched Lu tell Costa the story of interviewing sperm donors and Costa folded into their old listening posture from the detox, I saw myself curled and rambling out the story of my brother putting my stuff on the curb all those years ago, I saw Costa's listening for the first time for what it was, a vanishing act. One night Lu asked Costa what they knew about my childhood and they recited every fact I'd told them at the detox and when I blanched with exposure and surprise, Costa smiled at me and said, *be grateful, my love language is memorization.* I told Lu the hummingbird comment and she shrugged and said *I don't know people say weird stuff all the time* and when I told her the hummingbird comment was one of the cruelest things a person had ever said to me she looked me over from head to foot and said, *your problem is you take everything to heart.* So I could not sympathize with her when we got an email from Costa saying they'd been evicted and were driving to Montreal with their dog to stay with a friend, then nothing, same as always.

I used the Formula on my brother when he sent self-justifying texts about why he deserved the whole inheritance, it was mom's right to choose to leave me nothing, I used the Formula on a co-worker at the lab who sent vengeful texts after he was fired, every time I used the Formula I thought of Costa again and I wanted to write to them, tell them that whatever was going on I didn't care, whether it was detox or depression, it didn't matter to me, but I resisted, I am becoming a different person, I told myself, I am becoming a person who doesn't need to know and know and know, so I said nothing to their absence and their absence spoke back to me in tongues, but the Costa-worry pilot light at the base of my neck never went out, there was no stopping it, and when Lu gave birth a year later there was still nothing from Costa, I entered a tunnel of all-night walking, our son had colic, Lu's C-section incision got infected, healed, got infected and healed again, time became a shroud that blocked my body from windows and faces.

Star waving-hand dog and Costa was back, the text arrived the day before our son's first birthday, I showed Lu and she shrugged and said in a tired voice, *they're just going to let you down again, why do you want to get hurt*, I went out on the porch and curled up in the corner of the half-broken couch out there, gripped my knees and closed my eyes and allowed my chest to void of breath and fill back up with memories of Costa, and my phone vibrated and shouted in my hand with Costa's name, still recorded in my contacts as COSTA DETOX WORK FRIEND over a decade later, when I answered I put it on speakerphone to put distance between myself and their voice, when they began to speak my anger left me all at once. *I thought I should just call*, Costa's voice said, *I'm back on the coast, I need to know you're okay*, no apology, no explanation, nothing like that would ever come from Costa, *I'm doing better again, it was touch and go for awhile*, when our son called to a raven through the window where Lu stood eavesdropping there was a pause, *congratulations*, said Costa, we spoke for a couple hours.

My son's birthday party, I ran to the door, there was Costa in the cherrywood frame, shaved head, thick black beard, white jeans, their wide open eyes, an old argyle sweater I recognized from before, their embrace pressed all the bones in my body back into their correct places, while they held me I wondered why they were back and how long they would stay, then they walked around me into my home, dancing snow from their boots, and within a few minutes they'd filled a paper plate with red velvet cake and pineapple and had taken their place, cross-legged, on the couch beside Ike, turned and faced him, *you're Ike aren't you?*, said Costa, while Lu and I stared, Ike smiled uncertainly in his denim party blazer, and I watched my brother hug my brother and couldn't contain my tears when Costa set his palms around the back of Ike's skull and said, *I forgive you for everything.*

Petra Chambers

CONTAINMENT

Containment

Like any story, this story is attempting to be a container.

(…)

(I am the monster. I am the machine.)

(…)

ARTIFACT:

ENCULTURATION (age: 11)

1.

There was a time I believed in truth. Some things may still be true.

2.

It's true I found *Amnesty International Report on Torture* (1975) on my best friend's mother's bookshelf.

his deep roars. There were sympathetic quips and a shaking of heads and, after one long roar, someone added a soft, "In bed." They all knew him. Now Dale did too, not just the warrior honouring what he'd killed, but the man sacrificing himself for everyone.

Grant Buday

THE LIGHT NEVER SHUTS UP

Miroslav spent the first day aboard the *Abyssinia* vomiting. This was disappointing but not surprising. He'd vomited all the way across the Atlantic; why shouldn't he be sick in the Pacific? The second day he ceased vomiting because his gut, wrung dry, went into a permanent cramp and he could neither straighten out or sit up. On the third day the *Abyssinia* sighted an American whaler. The captains radioed back and forth. The American ship was short a hand so Miroslav was rolled in a tarp and slung across to the whaler in exchange for a jerry can of newly rendered oil.

The *Roosevelt* reeked of boiled blubber, the stench pervading decks and walls, the ceilings, the bunks, the bedding, the food, the crew, the very air itself. Miroslav, force-fed water, resumed his regimen of vomiting and cramping. Some days later—he would never know how many—he found himself aboard the *Cortes* bound for Acapulco. The *Cortes* had agreed to take him because he came with a case of whisky. In Acapulco he was put in a debtor's prison, for while it was true he'd not eaten a bite of food, he had consumed valuable stores of fresh water and ginger with which he had been dosed in a futile effort to turn him into a useful crewman.

In prison he caught malaria and thrashed so wildly he broke his bunk. This was interpreted as insubordination for which he was beaten with a bull-hide truncheon. A priest was brought in to administer last rites. Miroslav survived and was ordered released. The guard who had beaten him with such vigour picked him up under the armpits and towed him backward along the corridor—bare heels bumping over the worn brown bricks—and left him in the road. As fate would have it, the priest who had administered the last rites was passing. He told a pair of boys who were prodding Miroslav with bamboo sticks to stop what they were doing and carry him to the monastery, where he was sluiced with a pail of water and left to dry in a courtyard fragrant with flowering roses. Miroslav could only conclude that after spending time in Purgatory he had gone on to Heaven.

He was given his very own room. On the brick wall hung a crucified Christ rendered in wood by an artist with a loving eye for gruesome detail. Miroslav spent many hours admiring the craft and thinking of his own thwarted career as a carver of gravestones and monuments back in Bratislava before having been dragooned at the age of seventeen into the Kaiser's army to fight in World War I. Meals in the monastery consisted of garlic soup and dry bread served three times a day in a vaulted cavern reached by shallow steps. Miroslav's job was to scrub these steps each morning. In the afternoon he and Father Rodrigues sat beneath an avocado tree in a walled garden where the priest, smoking a cigar, described the many miracles he had witnessed in his distinguished career as a man of God. These included fish that climbed trees, doves flying from the mouths of nuns, mermaids riding seahorses, wounds healed by the spit of virgins, and, while on pilgrimage in the high sierras, red snow.

Miroslav could have done with some snow, red or white, for he found the Mexican heat crushing. Still, things were looking up. He was out of jail and he'd made a friend. He was also discovering fruit he'd never heard of much less eaten, including mango, papaya, and avocado. Father Rodrigues told him that avocado was the Nahuatl word for testicle. At first Miroslav thought he'd misheard, for the priest's English was heavily accented and Miroslav's basic.

"They must be giants," said Miroslav, hefting an avocado in his hand.

"No bigger than you," said the priest.

Miroslav asked if he'd ever heard of the yeti.

"Ah." Rodrigues smiled and nodded as if to say here was a tasty topic, and proceeded to speak at length of the great heads of eastern Mexico, relics of a race of giants.

"Statues?"

"No." The priest was adamant. "Petrified skulls."

"And they are there to this day?"

"Of course." The priest's eyes languidly closed and for a time the two men sat silent in the heat ringing with the sound of cicadas. Then Rodrigues was leaning toward Miroslav and regarding him with a lewd glint in his eye. "Come," he whispered. They went to a vine-obscured gate. Rodrigues unlocked it with a key he kept under his cassock. Glancing around, he gestured Miroslav through. With a finger to his lips signalling silence, the priest led the way along a colonnade lined with immense potted cacti. At another door overgrown with flowering vines, he invited Miroslav to peek through a gap in the planks. Nuns wading in a pond. This was not as exciting as it might have been given that all were wearing their full habits, though admittedly the wet cloth clung provocatively, and in some cases alarmingly. Under a balcony two chained mastiffs slept.

As Miroslav angled his head for a better view, a leaf tickled his nostril and he sneezed, not once but three times. The mastiffs leapt up barking. The wet nuns shrieked. Father Rodrigues fled with surprising speed. The mother superior had the gate open before Miroslav had recovered from his final sneeze and punched him in the forehead.

Despite Father Rodrigues's protestations, Miroslav found himself back in jail, this time sharing a cell with a Russian anarchist named Sergei. Due to the punch in the forehead, Miroslav now had an indentation stamped between his eyebrows shaped like a crucifix, the mother superior having been wearing a large signet ring in the form of their Saviour on the Cross. When it healed, this scar was such a perfect shape that one morning three guards came in, led by the one who had beaten him nearly to death, held Miroslav down, lit a candle, and filled the indentation with hot wax. Adding cold water to harden it, they then pried it out and went away laughing.

"You see," said Sergei, smiling with the serenity of the certain, "religion is shit." He showed Miroslav a bottle of gunpowder and a sack of nails. "The propaganda of the deed."

Miroslav had had enough propaganda in the war. As for deeds, he was inclined to think that the less you did the better. This view was reinforced the next night when the bomb went off taking with it a wall, the ceiling, and Sergei's right arm. Having taken to sleeping under his bunk on the stone floor because it was coolest spot in the cell, Miroslav emerged filthy but largely unscathed, and so it was therefore assumed that he must be the bomber. He was charged with various felonies. When Sergei died of his injury two days later, the charge of murder was added. He was sentenced to death by garrote.

Father Rodrigues visited to offer Christian solace.

"I'm innocent."

Rodrigues could not wholly agree. "We are all born with the taint of sin."

The priest left and Miroslav crawled under his bunk and lay in the fetal position.

The following morning the mother superior who had punched him and jailed him paid a visit. She was accompanied by the merciless guard, a surprisingly handsome man for one so cruel. Frowning and formal, he ordered Miroslav to come out from under his bunk.

Miroslav reluctantly obeyed. How black the mother superior's robe and how white her wimple. She had a long strong nose and smallpox scars on her cheeks, large and luminously dark eyes and a surprisingly fulsome mouth for one who had rejected life's sensual joys. She evaluated Miroslav, who by now weighed less than a hundred pounds, was coated in filth, smelled of latrine, and had tear stains cutting grooves down the dirt crusting his face. She told the guard, without turning to look at him, to leave. As disappointed as a dog deprived of its bone, he slunk scowling away.

"Do you believe in redemption?" Her English was precise, as if she was biting each word.

Redemption? Miroslav needed to think. Did it not imply that he had sinned?

"Forgiveness," she clarified.

Miroslav decided to grovel. He had grovelled often in the Kaiser's army. Dropping to his knees he bowed his face to the floor. As his forehead touched the gritty stone he recalled his crucifix-shaped scar and feared he was blaspheming and that as a result his garrotting would be preceded by a lengthy round of torture.

The mother superior said, "I am in a position to offer a pardon."

Still down on his hands and knees, Miroslav slowly raised his face and looked at her.

"A pardon in exchange for a service."

Miroslav waited.

"You will be my Apollo," which she pronounced *poyo*.

Poyo? Her chicken?

She saw his confusion. "You will take a message to the east."

He blinked then swallowed then nodded dumbly.

"Stand."

He stood.

"This is the message. Are you listening?"

Again he nodded.

The Mother Superior raised her right arm and, palm open, with the immense solemnity befitting her august status, she slapped him so hard across the face that he hit the floor.

*

Two days later Miroslav was riding a burro east into the mountains. The road, no more than a path, ran like a tunnel beneath a ceiling of trees whose branches met overhead. Birds whooped unseen. A flock of small green parrots plunged past like a fist full of flung stones. Vines drooped and mosses sagged. There were palms and creepers and ferns; everything rotted even as it grew, and the air was both sweet and rancid. As for the burro, it seemed to sleepwalk in a halo of flies.

Miroslav laughed. What a strange and alien sound in his ears. Not only had he escaped the garrotte, but he was wearing clean if second-hand clothes: sandals, breeches, shirt and vest, and sombrero, had eaten a full breakfast of coffee, eggs, and tortillas, had money in his pocket, and was travelling east toward the Olmec heads by way of Tabasco. Admittedly the message he was to deliver to the abbot of the monastery of Nuestra Senora de la Asuncion was troubling, but he would think of something. Perhaps he would simply not deliver it at all.

"I am trusting you," the Mother Superior had said.

Miroslav had nodded and put his hands together in the prayer position and thanked her, thanked her, thanked her. Now, on the mule, he thought: Fuck that old biddy; I shouldn't have been in jail in the first place.

On the third morning he was set upon by masked peasants who took his money then vanished into the forest. No idea what else to do, Miroslav continued on and not ten minutes later was surrounded again by those same thieves, only this time one stepped forward, a young woman with eyes like wet black pearls, and she returned half his money. "Para la revolución," she said. And once more they vanished into the forest.

As Miroslav rode on he found himself entranced by those black-pearl eyes gazing at him over her mask. Perhaps he should have offered to join? They could bring down the *corrupticos* and make love in the jungle. Instead, he must go and slap an abbot.

How he envied the certainty of the devout. Political or religious, their faith was like a key in a lock. The Kaiser's officers had had faith in the war. Sergei had faith in his bomb. Priests had faith in the crucifix. Miroslav had hoped that by travelling as far from Europe as possible he might find a place where faith was unnecessary. He touched the indentation between his eyebrows. It itched.

The landscape changed. He left the steaming jungle for the drier altitudes of rock and cactus. He reached Puebla de Zaragoza with its cobbled roads, high walls with iron-barred windows, its cathedrals as well as motorcars and autobuses that pumped black smoke. In a plaza he saw stone angels, their bare breasts round and perfect, their wings upraised as they took flight. He dismounted the burro and walked among the figures. Following the noise of steel chipping stone, he entered a shop and found an old man at work on a block of marble. Miroslav began that day. How good it felt to hold a chisel again. He ran his thumb over the ridges of the rasp, ran his palm over the curve of stone.

"There is an angel inside," said Don Miguel. "You must let her out."

Don Miguel's face was a landscape of narrow valleys and low hills silted with stone dust. The only moisture about him was in his eyes, two muddy pools reddened by decades of grit. The shop was cool, with a packed dirt floor and a high ceiling supported by ceiba posts on which tools were hung from loops of leather. As Don Miguel's English was limited and Miroslav's Spanish basic, they often worked hours at a stretch without speaking, the only sounds the chink-chink of the chisels and the scrape of the files and the muted murmur of the world outside broken only by the periodic bells of the Catedral de los Martir. Don Miguel slept in the shop and allowed Miroslav to do the same. Miroslav often lay awake. Everything was good, which meant it must soon turn bad, which meant he worried. The Mother Superior was not naive. Had she alerted all the religious houses en route? Were all the monks and nuns reporting his progress? Or more importantly, his lack of progress?

Each morning Miroslav swept out the mouse droppings then boiled the coffee while Don Miguel looked at the slab of marble. Most of the headstones were near the front of the shop where the light was best, and some were outside for display. One particular slab, however, was positioned so that it got both the morning sunlight from the east window and the evening light from the west window.

"Esta es la luz que habla," said Don Miguel.

Miroslav picked his way through the translation: *This is the light that speaks*. "And what does it say, this light?"

"It tells me who is inside."

Miroslav regarded the slab. It was about seven feet high and three wide and two deep. It looked like a stone door. Except there was no room onto which it opened. He wondered if perhaps Don Miguel spent too much time with his angels. For about a quarter of an hour in the morning the slab cast a shadow and Don Miguel stood between the slab and the light so that his own shadow fell upon it. In the evening he did the same but from the other side.

"How long has it been here?" asked Miroslav.

"Seven years. They are growing impatient."

"Who?"

"The priests."

"But the light has not spoken?"

Don Miguel shook his head. "The light never shuts up."

Miroslav thought about this all day as he worked. In the evening, when the light briefly angled through the opposite window, Don Miguel once more stood before the slab regarding his silhouette upon the stone.

"When will you begin work?"

Tired after the day, Don Miguel put his gnarly old hands upon Miroslav's shoulders and positioned him between the window and the slab so that his shadow fell upon it.

"You do it. You're the one it has been waiting for."

"Me?"

"You." And Don Miguel touched the scar on Miroslav's brow.

Fearful, Miroslav tried to hear the voice of the light. Again he wondered if the old man had been breathing too much stone dust. As he stood there between the slab of stone and the light of the setting sun, Miroslav watched his silhouette vanish slowly from the legs up. When it was gone it seemed that others remained, flickering briefly like flame shadows.

"Which one do I let out?"

"Exactly," said Don Miguel, for that was the challenge.

The next day a priest appeared. His hat was as flat as a soup plate, his eyes, which never blinked, were holes bored in stone.

"Soon," said Don Miguel. "Very soon."

The priest went away, though not before looking long at Miroslav as if memorizing his face with its strange scar.

That evening Miroslav stood before the stone slab. It had now been three months since he'd left Acapulco. The dry season was upon them and the air had a welcome chill at night so that he needed a blanket. He thought about the message he was to deliver. Was he dishonourable for failing to complete his mission? Was honour the solace he'd have after slapping the abbot and being thrown in jail yet again and this time left to rot? Or would the abbot slap Miroslav and say take that message back across the country to the Mother Superior? And so he would go back and forth like a pendulum. He picked up his hammer and chisel and positioned himself so that his silhouette fell upon the slab. Then he stepped aside. Was he not merely inflicting his own shape upon the stone? Striding forward he struck the slab on the very top. Nothing. He looked at Don Miguel, who was watching intently. Miroslav gripped the hammer more tightly. What had he been expecting—one blow and a husk of stone would fall revealing the figure of a beautiful woman? Setting his hammer and chisel aside, he put his palms to the slab and began to caress it all over. It was coarse in places and smooth in others, and cold, very cold. His face was hot so he pressed his brow to the stone; finally he embraced it, letting it take his heat even as he absorbed its chill.

In the morning he shook Don Miguel's hand and said he would return as soon as possible. Then he looked at the slab. He had worked all night and revealed the face within—the Mother Superior, eyes closed, expression enigmatic, as if listening.

He remounted his burro. As he descended the eastern slope of the mountains the jungle heat rose around him. It took two weeks to reach the monastery of Nuestra Senora de la Asuncion. He arrived during the lull of midday. Nothing moved. Only the cicadas continued their relentless rasping. The monastery was outside the city, and three times Miroslav lifted the great iron ring and let it fall. Eventually a pair of eyes appeared in a slat-sized window.

"I have a message from Acapulco for the abbot."

"Tell me."

"I must deliver it myself."

The eyes watched him. Was the abbot wary of visitors with messages? The slat was shut and the slow clanking process of unlatching the great door began. Miroslav followed the monk to a courtyard. From the branches of an avocado tree hung wire cages containing canaries but none sang. There was an enormous stillness, as if the world was far away. Miroslav saw the appeal of such peace; it felt as if eternity was here.

Eventually he heard a distant door, footsteps, then a second door. An elderly though upright man appeared. Miroslav thought of a man returning from the past, a man communing with saints a thousand years old.

"I am Father Antonio." He was pale, silver-haired, clean-shaven, in a heavy dark robe, a fine silver chain around his neck dangling a crucifix no bigger than a thumbnail. He had thick cheeks and clear eyes and he stood with his hands clasped behind his back. A scent of cool earth emanated from him. The birds in the cages began to twitter; one sang a long high note that ended in a trill. Father Antonio's gaze went past Miroslav to the bird, to the song, and he smiled as though all was reaffirmed. Returning his gaze to Miroslav he said, "You have the communication." His English was slow, and not so much a question as a statement of fact. Had he been waiting? Was he angry? But he seemed beyond anger. His scent of cool earth was clean, like a wind moving across a freshly plowed field, a landscape that had never known blood or fire.

Miroslav began to tremble. How was he to raise his arm and strike this man? What a fool he'd been to think he could do such a thing. He thought of the revolutionary in the jungle. He thought of the slab in Don Miguel's workshop. What an outrageous task the Mother Superior had given him.

"I will not condemn the messenger," the priest assured him.

Miroslav raised his right hand and, with a groan, thinking of his years marching on blistered feet in the Kaiser's war, recalling the stench of dead horses bloating in ditches, the laments of the dying, the rage of the officers, the smell of garlic and gun oil, the vinegary stink of sweat and fear, he cried out and swung his hand as hard as he could. The priest turned his face because at that moment the bird sang again and Miroslav missed, and yet his momentum carried him forward into the priest's arms. How long he remained there in his embrace he did not know but he made no effort to move, the smell of cool earth in his nose, bird-song in his ears, the silver crucifix fitting perfectly into the scar on his brow.

Shashi Bhat

KEEPING THINGS FRESH

Your life, little girl, is an empty page that
men will want to write on.
—"Sixteen Going on Seventeen," *The Sound of Music*

She has begun reading the American newspapers, and she has already learned about so many new things. It isn't easy to get through a dense article on an unfamiliar subject, but she takes it slowly, consulting the occasional flow chart or Wikipedia article. It is a good time for learning about this country: there's an election coming. Today alone she has read about mortgage-backed securities, US-Cuba relations, and the resurgence of cube steak. Having grown up in a vegetarian household, she had never even heard of cube steak, and would not have been able to identify it at a meat counter. But the *New York Times* had helpful pictures, and after reading of "greasy, grim casseroles studded with string beans," and that "cube steak represented all that was unstylish and lacking," she understood its history, and how far it had come, and why it had regained popularity—because of the economy, of course, and now she knows all about that, too.

She cooks up some cube steak, taking cues from the article to sauté it in butter and season with just a little salt and pepper. Her boyfriend seems surprised when she serves it for dinner, since she usually makes smoky, earthy legumes and rustic, grainy breads, but he also seems awed at how much and how quickly she is learning.

"Look at my little vegetarian," he says, and admires the dish rack, where she has nimbly balanced more dishes than would have seemed possible given the rack's size. "This bodes well for your future wifely abilities," he says.

"Let's eat in front of the TV," she suggests, knowing he expects her to switch on a sitcom rerun, but instead she chooses the nightly news. They watch it together, and she nods in all the right places.

*

When the election rolls around, she keeps notes of the various candidates' platforms and streams the live debates on CNN.com. Because she shares Wi-Fi with the neighbours, the connection is spotty and once in a while the screen freezes, capturing John McCain with his hands and mouth spread wide, and she panics and disconnects and reconnects until the feed jerks back into pixelated life.

That week she leaves open the map that shows Electoral College votes in each state, refreshing and refreshing, a knot in her throat. This is what it is like to participate in democracy.

A couple of months later, she catches a bus to DC with her boyfriend at 3 a.m. to attend Obama's inauguration, and while watching on a big screen, crammed in with thousands of others on the National Mall, American flags painted on their cheeks, she is moved to tears, even though she is only in the US on a student visa and thus doesn't have a vote.

*

In the spring, out to dinner at a Mexican restaurant with her boyfriend and meeting his parents for the first time, she manages to mention the recent suffering of domestic catfish farming due to the rising prices of corn and soybean. "It's really a symbol of a complex economy," she says, and continues to discuss the politics of high-fructose corn syrup with the boyfriend's father, who nods vigorously as he loads a chip with pico de gallo.

Afterwards, she is alone with the boyfriend, sitting on his lap in his apartment's single damaged armchair, and he tells her that his father was impressed.

"You're really doing well with all of this," her boyfriend says.

"I feel like Eliza Doolittle," she replies in a very accurate Cockney accent.

"Wait, who's that again?" he asks.

"Eliza Doolittle? From *My Fair Lady*?" She should have said *Pygmalion.* It would've been a good chance for her to prove again that she isn't some dummy. And besides that, she favours Shaw's original ending for *Pygmalion.* She doesn't like the ending of *My Fair Lady* at all. "Maybe you should read *Pygmalion*," she could've said.

It wasn't like she hadn't known anything before she moved to this country and started this whole newspaper endeavour. Was it five months ago? Yes, five months ago her boyfriend had sent her that text message—*can we talk 5min yr apt*—and he'd shown up to her cramped studio sobbing. He pushed past her into her apartment, and she followed him, bewildered, and sat down on the bed as he paced across the tiny room, then tried to pull out of him what was wrong. The way he was behaving she thought his whole family had died, or he had irrevocably bashed somebody in the head and the authorities were coming for him and now he would never be able to finish his master's thesis. He kneeled as though in supplication, grasping her legs, while burying his face in her blankets. She finally got it out of him that he was crying because he intended to break up with her, and she prodded: "Why?"

And then he listed the reasons: "You talk too much about flowers... You have a hair growing on your areola and it makes me uncomfortable to see that on a woman... You watch too many sitcom reruns and it's like you aren't aware of serious artists. For example, I don't think you've ever seen a Woody Allen movie... You sometimes talk about your problems like they are more important than mine... You don't know anything about American politics... If my friends heard you talking, I just don't think they'd see you as an intellectual..." This went on for approximately twenty minutes.

She'd replied, slowly, thoughtfully: "You think I'm stupid."

"I don't," he said. "Just, you know."

This was the first person she had ever slept with. *Dumb, dumb, dumb*, he must have been thinking, as he fucked her. She loved him severely, for no good reason. Her father would not have liked him. But she thought of the empty summer ahead, in this bleak, scorching city. Of all the activities they had planned that would be cancelled. She didn't really have any friends on this side of the ocean. It was just her and nobody else. Years later, she will think of this as the moment that split her life in two.

Her eyes wandered to the single purple hyacinth she had stolen from a public garden six weeks ago and placed in a clean jam jar on her bedside table. The flower's tight blooms resembled the curls of Marge Simpson's hair. She had plucked it not for its looks but for the intensity of its fragrance: an invitation to breathe deeply. A reminder to get enough air.

"I know there are things I need to work on... I'll try," she vowed. "Really. I'll start reading the *New York Times*. I can trim that hair. Woody Allen, got it." She didn't say anything about the flowers.

"I could give you a list," he said helpfully.

And so he'd wiped his tears on her comforter, which he then threw off the bed so they could make love passionately and tenderly and also intelligently.

*

After her boyfriend went home that night, she couldn't sleep. It was as though he had bought a house and wanted it renovated, and she was both the contractor and the house itself, which was red when he chose it, but now he'd prefer it painted blue, and maybe a new electrical system, and she was the painter and the electrician and the yard maintenance worker, as well.

So she typed up an email in defence—*I am not some blank robot who needs to be programmed, but I, like everyone else, am a work-in-progress, and I need you to understand that*—and she provided a rundown of her accomplishments, such as speaking seven languages fluently, founding a million-dollar flower delivery business while still a teenager, winning a national medal for entrepreneurship, and receiving a scholarship to attend a top school in America after her only living parent was killed in a train derailment. Before she sent the message, she attached her resumé as a biting punchline.

She checked her email every three minutes. Standing up and going to the fridge and opening the door to stare inside and coming back and checking her email. Going to the bathroom and sniffing a bar of soap and coming back and checking her email. Folding one shirt and coming back and checking her email.

Then, the subject line in bold, unread. She opened the message. His response said, *You're hired!* And several lines down: *God, that email really made me love you.*

*

She decided she would take some of his suggestions anyway. It would be like getting Botox or learning new positions from *Cosmo*—it would keep things fresh, give her something new to talk about, and probably wouldn't hurt that much. And now she knows the latest US unemployment statistics, where to find the best deals on auto insurance, which brand of bottled water conserves the most packaging, and that *Watchmen* had divided critical opinion. But *Watchmen* has left the theatres, so she consults the reviews for another movie he had seen and recommended, but in a few weeks that is gone too—everything is out of date and everybody has moved on, because now there is an earthquake, an ash cloud, a health-care plan, a climate bill, an oil spill, a documentary about babies.

*

Six years ago: she was standing inside a television studio, about to pitch her company on her country's reality investment show. The show was not unlike *Shark Tank*, she would tell her boyfriend-turned-fiancé later, in a second life. Quieter, though. Less bombastic. Less colour and less sound. The set was a simple grey room. The investors sat in four brown leather armchairs in a spaced-out row at the other end, facing her. Beside each chair was a small table with a glass of water, a notepad, and a pen. To the right: bright lights, a camera crew. Later they would add a narrative voice-over and broadcast it on her country's one publicly funded channel.

As she began to speak, her voice did not quaver. "I'm asking for two hundred thousand dollars for a twenty percent stake in my company." The two friends she had recruited to help her walked out in pressed white blouses and black skirts, each carrying a vase of flowers, which they placed on the investors' tables. There were four mixed bouquets of cream-coloured peonies, yellow roses, green button pompon chrysanthemums, Italian ruscus, and seeded eucalyptus.

She told the investors about her business: a flower delivery service. Working with local growers, she prepared arrangements and sold them to businesses and individuals using a subscription model. To deliver the product, she had hired other girls from her school, who rode around town on their bicycles with flowers spilling out of the front baskets. It was like Uber, but with bicycles and flowers instead of cars and passengers, except that Uber didn't yet exist.

Before coming here, she had researched the investors to find out if any of them suffered from seasonal allergies. This information was not publicly available, but thankfully, they all seemed to possess underactive immune systems. The investor in the chair farthest to the left was a man who one might argue was both too thin and too rich. He was like a willow tree that grew money. Next to him was the investor who had been on the show the longest—her father's favourite, because of the book he'd written about becoming a millionaire incrementally by investing the loose change left over at the end of each day. The book made a million dollars sound possible, her father had said. The third man had made his fortune with a Brazilian fast-food chain and could really pull off a pocket square. In the fourth chair was the lone woman—the newest investor on the show, who had built a tech empire and often spoke in terms the others couldn't follow, though they nodded along. She wore the same gold suit the whole season, for visual consistency, because the filming schedule was such that they spliced pitches from different days into each episode. The men wore identical black or grey suits every day, but that was less remarkable.

"Now, tell us your sales figures," commanded the money-willow man.

"And are you taking a salary for yourself?" inquired the loose-change man.

"How much have you spent on marketing?" queried the pocket-square man.

"Who handles the back end on the e-commerce site?" asked the woman in gold.

"What are your net profits?"

"How much of your own money have you put into this?"

"What are you paying those delivery girls?"

"What is your average customer acquisition cost?"

They pinged and she ponged. She knew her numbers. Over many nights, she had stayed up late with one friend or another quizzing her, while she pinched the neck of a rose and scraped the thorns off its stem with a knife. *Know your numbers*, her father had always told her when she was six years old and they watched this show on the black-and-white television in their kitchen, so small the investors' faces were like coins. At the time, she could recite multiplication tables from one to ten, which she practised while her father chopped potatoes and put them on the stove to boil. *Don't waste anyone's time* was another one of her father's adages, so before the show she had prepared a flowery introduction full of all her best puns, and ruthlessly pruned it; distilled it like rosewater.

Early that morning she had arranged the bouquets and set them in buckets lined with Styrofoam inside the rear of the van. While she drove, a friend sat in back, embracing the flowers so they wouldn't tip over as the van bumped over potholed streets on the way to the studio. Before carrying them inside, the girls used small loops of Scotch tape to stick on each vase a business card in matte tangerine. *Kew Gardens*, it said, in a white serif font. She had ordered the cards from a fledgling family-owned printshop in her town, and after that they became permanent customers. The name referred to a Virginia Woolf story she had read, where a variety of flawed people stroll through an omniscient London garden.

Next, the investors asked about margins. About the price point and how it compared to her competitors.

"That seems a bit high," said the woman in gold. "How are you able to charge this much?"

"Who knew there was so much money in flowers?" mused pocket-square.

"Who are your customers?" questioned loose-change.

Her customers were serene restaurants and bustling cafés, sleek law and counselling offices, modest households, and dedicated lovers.

"Even if people will pay that much, there's still an issue here," remarked money-willow. "None of this is proprietary. What's to keep someone else from starting an identical business and stealing all your customers?"

There was a twist. Something she hadn't yet told them.

"Those flowers next to you," she said. Her friends, who were standing to one side, hands clasped tightly in front of them, snuck glances at each other, trying to hide their excitement. "Those flowers were cut six weeks ago."

"Six weeks?" The woman in gold raised a single eyebrow.

"What do you mean?" wondered loose-change. "Do flowers usually last that long?" He turned to the woman for confirmation.

"They look as though they were picked this morning." Pocket-square rubbed the petal of the peony closest to him between his thumb and forefinger, as though testing to see if it were real.

She raised her hand up to eye level, holding a tablet the size of a dime. It was round, pastel pink, and chalky. The investors craned their necks and squinted to see. "We add this to the water." She dropped it in a glass of water she had on the display table in front of her, and it hissed as it dissolved. "It's non-toxic," she told them. "You could drink the water in those vases if you wanted to, and it would soothe acid reflux and taste like strawberry soda. The flowers last for a minimum of six weeks." It was a formula she had discovered by serendipity and then perfected. The ingredients were the price of wheat. And she owned the patent.

"If you're doing so well, why do you need our help?"

"To expand," she told them. At present she produced the tablets at home in her kitchen, but with the investment, she could outsource manufacturing. And bicycle delivery could only go so far.

"I don't know anything about flowers. But my money is on *you*," said loose-change, pointing at her without smiling. "You, I can tell, will get things done."

All four of them invested. It was a first in the show's history.

The episode would play forever in syndication.

*

She is sitting with her fiancé-turned-new-husband, here in their usual café with the big ceramic cups and Dave Brubeck playing from staticky speakers and the dim, flattering lighting that had allowed them to fall in love (their first date had been here). They are arguing over a quote, what that politician's wording had been when he stated his belief about pregnancies resulting from rape—she knows he said, "If it's a legitimate rape, the female body has ways to try to shut that whole thing down..." but her husband disagrees. What is odd is that they are on the same side—they both know what the man said was absurd; it is only the exact words they can't agree on, but the words as he remembers them don't sound as awful somehow. Her husband had laughed about the statement, because to him what stands out is the man's stupidity and the nebulous way he spoke with no evidence, as though science were just a cloud of guesses. And this bothers her, too—imagine thinking a body had insight, could make the right decisions, that a body knew what love is and isn't. She wishes it did. But what is worse is the man's staggering callousness, his dismissal of the whole fate of a woman. To her husband the issue is theoretical and distant, but to her those words are like being gutted with a wrench.

And anyway, he is wrong, he is definitely wrong. "No, you're wrong," she insists, and needs so badly to prove it that she is near tears with frustration, and she can prove it, too, because though neither of them has a smartphone (he believes smartphones are a distraction from the present moment), she has that section of the newspaper right here in her handbag (they had switched to a paper subscription because he prefers the old-fashioned dignity of newsprint). So she reaches into the handbag, rattling the ChapStick and pens to pull out the folded, rolled paper, but her water bottle has leaked, wetting the page she wanted; she holds the page in her hand and estimates its new worth.

That night they eat the meal of fattoush and chickpea salad she prepared—they are both vegetarians now (he had watched a documentary about factory farming). "Should we have sex?" he asks, as he tends to after he has eaten a light dinner and gone on a half-mile digestive stroll.

"I guess so," she says.

"Have you...?" he nods in the general direction of her lower half. He has a strong dislike for body hair, perhaps because he is naturally as hairless as a ball of mozzarella. Her own dark hair coats her whole body—she is constantly tweezing, and who knows how much of her money has gone to wax? He also prefers when she sprinkles a scented powder in her undergarments, so everything smells vaguely of roses, the most overrated of flowers.

She shakes her head.

"It's okay this one time," he says, with an air of generosity.

The mattress needs replacing. He raises her hips for better leverage. It is always when they're in bed, when she's pressed like a petal under his hairless body, that she feels it most acutely: the weight of her choices and his preferences. She has lived two lives: one active and one passive. One where she has ideas and crafts them into living things. One where she is erased by someone else's shallow desires. One magic and one ordinary. One full and fruitful, where time is elastic, and one where she is wilting by the day, by the second. He lifts her leg mechanically, like a chiropractor. Adjusts and arranges her.

She remembers walking home after the TV show appearance, after returning the van, holding a large leftover bouquet wrapped in a newspaper she hadn't read. On the street headed towards her was a homeless man she recognized from town. He opened his arms wide and grinned: "For me?"

On impulse, she had thrust the whole bunch at him. "For you!" she said, because she had so much to give. There are no flowers in her house. Her husband is allergic. But there are flowers on the wallpaper of the café where they met, flowers that hold her attention like hindsight, like a premonition of the past. She examines them every time she's there, silently chanting, *Hydrangea. Gladiola. Chrysanthemum.* She can name every single one.

*

Before she left for America, she transferred part ownership of the flower business to the friends who had helped her. Now, a decade and a half has passed, and their success has been extraordinary. *Business is blooming!* it says on the news section of their website, which she checks late at night after drinking a glass of wine and while pumping her breast milk, as her husband sleeps nearby. She still owns the patent and a percentage of the company's shares and collects dividends that pay their mortgage and her husband's student loans. *He isn't so bad,* she thinks. *He isn't so bad*. Her husband is just a choice she made, one branch of a river with infinite tributaries that all empty into the same sea.

*

After the loans are paid off and her sons have moved out, she will leave her husband, and with the money she has left after the divorce, she will rent an apartment on her own, where she will grow flowers and body hair and rediscover the gentle sitcoms she watched in her youth. She will adopt a Persian cat and speak to it only in French and Italian. And because no news will appear on her screen or arrive at her door, she will forget what day it is, what month, what year. One evening she will crouch in front of an ancient VCR, put in a recording, and press *Play*. Four investors looming in front of her young self. Narrow shoulders in a white blouse. The sweat between her shoulder blades, and the radiant tenor of her own proud voice. Numbers playing in her head like a song.

"I don't know anything about flowers. But my money is on *you*," says her father's favourite investor, who built a fortune from a single coin. He is pointing at her, voice urgent as a train.

"I agree," says the woman in gold, who is dead now, and who always got the last word. "You could do anything you wanted."

D. F. McCourt

ONE WAY OUT

Loading game file...
Loaded.

This island exists. It causes the world and is caused by it. Cascading rivers carve it free from the ancient shales and sandstones of the lowlands. Maples and tamaracks—chanterelles and blackberries sprouting up at their ankles—spring forth on the slopes of the great hills. Raccoons wash autumn's hoarded acorns in the springtime creeks of snowmelt, while barred owls dive for voles in the young stalks of maize. This makes sense.

One Way Out
An Interactive Fiction by Jessica Sharp (published May 3, 1994)
Release 1 / Serial number 138203 / IFparser 4 build 17.01rl02

You are on a residential street in Verdun, on the island of Montreal. The summer sun hangs low in the sky, glinting off windshields of roadside cars—their bumpers dinged by decades of inexpert parallel parking—and illuminating clouds of gnats lurking in the shade of honey-locusts. The River St. Lawrence froths into rapids on the far side of the park to south. The Canals L'Aqueduc and Lachine—and your destination beyond—lie somewhere to the north.

You can hear a faint tune on the air, ethereal, lilting.

> Go north

You walk towards the setting sun, squinting your eyes against the intensity of the rays as they cut through the cool autumn air. By the time you cross the bridge over the Canal L'Aqueduc, you are rubbing your hands together against the chill. You wish you'd brought a jacket, but it's too late to turn back. You don't want to miss the show.

> The sun is setting in the north? And wasn't it summer a second ago?

I understood "explain the sun setting in the north" and "explain the changing seasons."

This is Montreal. North is west. Summer is winter. Time and space are not your friends. You get used to it.

> Go north

You reach the Lachine Canal just as the sun is dipping below the horizon. A numbing wind cuts through your thin clothes. From the bridge, you can see snow blowing in dusty eddies across the flat frozen surface of the canal. You keep moving. The playhouse is just ahead, a bastion of warmth, community, and storytelling. You have arrived.

> Enter playhouse

Winter jackets are draped haphazardly on the backs of folding chairs before an intimate little stage hung with no real set dressing. You dodge gritty salt-streaked puddles of boot melt on your way to an empty seat by the front. The skin on your arms stings and itches as you begin to thaw from your journey. A young man and woman extricate themselves from the small gathered crowd and step up onto the stage. Brother and sister, it is obvious, now that you look more closely.

They introduce themselves as Annick and François Tremblay. And then, in an instant, the show has begun.

The footfalls of the players beat an arrhythmic tattoo on the stage, primal, discordant.

> Watch show

I'm afraid it's entirely in French. Which you don't understand, despite having lived in Montreal for years.

> Explain show

I'll give you the gist of it.

You cause the world and are caused by it. Everything neat and measurable on both sides of the equation, or how could it ever balance? This makes sense.

But what of hope? Of despair? Desire, regret, meaning? They weigh nothing. They have no levers for cause nor traction for effect. They don't make sense. But they are you.

Don't call it a soul. Call it a tether. A sacred cloud half in this world and half in another altogether. Your being is a filament of magic that reaches beyond this flat reality into the infinite dimensionality of the sublime.

You are not a thing. You are a song. But mind your tune. Watch your volume. Because the chords you strike in this world play also in that other incomprehensible place. And you know not what circles overhead. How sharp its ears. How hungry it may be for a noisy vole in the unmaize.

> Isn't that a bit high-concept for community theatre?

I understood "please bring it down to my level."

Okay.

The story begins in 1823. Hundreds of mostly Irish migrant workers are labouring in the muddy trenches of what will become the Lachine Canal, an ambitious navigable ribbon across the island of Montreal, bypassing the rapids and connecting the Atlantic to the great inland lakes.

Shovel by shovel and pick by pick, the island is scarified. On stage, the players take turns as diggers, as blasters, as heavy horses clouding the air with hot breath as they haul away ton upon ton of excavated dirt and shale. Until, here, one of these shovels unearths a broken artifact.

Two halves that fit together to form a perfect sphere of fired clay, the size of a billiard ball and adorned all around with strange markings that the worker is unsurprised to find indecipherable.

He can read neither English nor French, and is only dimly aware that other languages might have existed here. He hands the orb off to one of the engineers who in turn sells it to a parish priest of Notre Dame.

The priest, unnamed and played with haughty disdain by Annick, fancies himself somewhat of a scholar on Iroquoian cultures, but the clay sphere is as opaque to him as it was to the Irish labourer.

The players, as sun and moon, circle the cathedral as the new basilica is built up behind it, rendered in an inspired bit of puppetry. In 1830, the sphere, along with the priest, moves into the new structure and the old building is demolished. Time spins around the basilica as the city burgeons. In 1847, the priest contracts typhus from a newly arrived parishioner and is among the first to succumb in the epidemic that follows.

In 1868, amid a push to make room for construction of a new pipe organ, the keeperless sphere is bundled up with a great salmagundi of other artifacts and crated off to a museum. There, the curator, played posh and Anglo by François, is briefly fascinated before joining the legacy of the bewildered. The markings on the sphere are not any known language and they do not match any documented Haudenosaunee artistic tradition. The curator does, at least, manage to date the artifact to the mid-eighteenth century, far too recent to garner any significant academic interest.

It is a curio, a toy, the unimportant work of some idle artisan without vision or schooling. Unfit for display, it is catalogued and archived. Inert.

Until, in 1962, a routine photographing of the collection captures its image, reproducing it in the pages of a minor specialist quarterly publication. So propagated, the signal reaches new eyeballs, new minds, all but one of which skate over it without finding purchase.

That one is Yves-Michel Tremblay, prodigy in the young field of data science, grandfather of Annick and François. Yves-Michel, played with dignity by Annick, makes pilgrimage to the museum and entreats the successor of the successor of the successor of the original curator (all indistinguishably François) for a closer look.

So ends act one.

> Explain salmagundi

Really? That's what you're stuck on? It's a dish of chopped meat, fish, eggs, pickles, and onions. You know, a hodgepodge.

> Leave playhouse

It would be rude to exit in the middle of the show. Don't you want to know what happens next?

> Haunted Indigenous artifact. I've seen this one before. It's all a bit othering and appropriative, wouldn't you say?

I understood "I am too smart and cultured for this."

Very good. You don't need to hear what happened to Yves-Michel. Of course your assumptions are all correct. This story is exactly what you think it is.

You leave the playhouse.

The sun is rising in the south. The streets are empty and the air is knives. Second winter is upon the city. You will not survive long outside in your summer clothes.

You hear a click as the doors of the little theatre lock behind you.

You feel a tuneless cadence vibrating into your feet from the frozen pavement, insatiable, menacing.

> Go south

Your limbs are anchors by the time you reach the Lachine Canal. You can no longer feel your fingers, nor your face. Your lips have cracked in the cold and every breath ravages your lungs.

There is frozen blood on the canal. You fall to your knees and then into a seated slump against a young white cedar. As your heart begins to slow, your thoughts stretch and attenuate into senselessness. It is a comfortable place to rest.

The wind carries a faint tune, ancient, haunting. This music is the final visitor to your sensorium. It shuts the door on the way out.

> The end?

No.

You are William Thatch, an erstwhile toymaker's apprentice from Surrey, lured across the sea by promises of glory serving the king's army in the eviction of the French from the colonies. Glory was a hectic whirlwind of violence on the Plains of Abraham, where you fired but once, wide into the low-hanging branches of a tree, before taking a musket ball in the leg. You were awarded a small plot of land in Côte-Saint-Paul on the island of Montreal for your patriotism and sacrifice. It is the Year of our Lord, 1766.

Your stomach is full with a breakfast of bread, eggs, jam, and a cold slice of yesterday's roast. Your wife Marie Angélique is washing up and preparing to mend a pair of little Joseph's breeches when you quit the house for the morning. You kick your lame leg twice against the crooked gatepost on your way past, a ritual flagellation intended to inspire obedience in the damned limb throughout the day to come. It rarely works.

You want nothing more on this fine spring morning than to ensconce yourself straight away in your workshop and tinker with your latest creation, a tin mechanical duck that flaps its wings when you press down on its bill. For days you've been puzzling over whether it might be possible to fit some manner of small noisemaker inside and, if so, how best to reproduce the earthy warbling call of the hooded merganser.

Alas, first your legs, good and bad both, must carry you over the hill to the eastern reaches of the estate, where your younger brother Benedict—newly arrived from England and as yet unwed—yesterday reported sighting a vagrant wagon encamped at the stand of beeches beside the creek. Your Tower of London horse pistol hangs from your belt, though purely for show. You haven't bothered bringing powder and you aren't even certain the old thing would fire anymore, so long has it been since you used it. Still, the sight of it should be enough to move along a roamer, even borne as it is by a cripple. With luck, you might be assessing the sounds of ratchet mechanisms for duckness by midmorning.

You can hear a faint tune drifting over the fields, foreign, unwelcome.

> This makes sense

Very clever.

> Go east

Sure enough, as you crest the hill you can see a figure sat next to a pit of embers at the creekside. Under the beeches stands a decrepit wagon and an even more decrepit donkey.

Drawing closer, you are struck by how loose the man's sun-baked skin sits on his old bones. A tide of charity wells up within you.

"These are my lands you're camped on, friend," you say. "But there's still planting left to do if you're willing to work for food and perhaps a little coin."

The roamer pays you no mind, just hums a tuneless refrain, the same uncanny song you heard on the wind before. Annoyed, you step closer and speak louder. "I said—"

The man looks up at you then, with blank eyes that suck all light from the morning. He draws his lips back in a horrific gap-toothed grin and solemnly taps his ear with his finger.

> Tap gun

Well, you tried. With a sigh, you return his gesture by tapping the butt of the horse pistol.

This, the deaf man seems to understand. With little fuss, he kicks dirt over the cinders of his fire and begins to hitch the weary donkey, humming all the while. You can't imagine the beast will be able to pull that load much farther before God takes it.

>Inventory

You have:

A Tower of London horse pistol (in your belt, unloaded)

Three Spanish reales and an old French écu (in your pocket)

> Give man coin

Guiltily, you dig a French silver écu from your pocket and toss it to him. Plenty to lease a bed and fill a belly for a couple of nights at the public house in Verdun, should he head that way. You'll need to forget to mention this largess to Marie Angélique, as she wouldn't abide such sentimentality. But surely, you reassure yourself, the king will soon enough get his affairs in order and proper currency will reign in these parts anyhow.

The man pockets the coin with a barking laugh and scrambles aboard his wagon. You watch as the dismal caravan lurches along the creek toward the road.

> Go west

On your way back to the workshop, you find your leg stretching out nicely and your spirits lifted by your own generosity. All jollity is banished however, when you notice a long stretch of fence fallen and trampled along the northern line. Wagon tracks run unapologetic across the fallen planks. Damn that vagrant, you curse under your breath. If you had two good legs, you'd be of a mind to chase him down, take back your écu, and march him straight back here at gunpoint to do the repairs.

Sadly, even a half-dead donkey outpaces you these years. Instead, you lose the rest of the day fixing the fence yourself.

As you work, you catch yourself singing snatches of the roamer's fool song despite yourself. It lacks any appreciable rhythm or melody, as is to be expected from a deaf man's ditty, you suppose. Still, something in its structure is intoxicating, keeps it bubbling to your lips unbidden.

> Go to workshop

As you attempt to stealthily approach the workshop door, you lament for the hundredth time having built the thing within line of sight of the kitchen window.

"I think not," Marie Angélique calls sternly from the house. "Supper is nearly ready."

Over a plate of stew and mash, you find yourself hoping benevolently that, despite his sins, the deaf man and his sad beast have found their way to a hearty meal as well.

After supper, while Marie Angélique is clearing the table, Joseph—three years old next week—plays on the floor with a train you made for him when he was still too young to hold it. He looks up at you as though sensing your gaze.

"Lève-moi, papa."

"In English, boy," you say, standing and lifting him into your arms. "I didn't risk my hide in that war to have my son speaking French at me."

Marie Angélique scoffs and raises an eyebrow at you. "Well, you will have to spend more time with him then, no? Bring him to the workshop with you tomorrow. He would love to watch you work. You can speak English at him all day."

"The workshop, Ange? Do you not realize how much trouble a child could find in there? He could lose a finger."

"He has ten, no? Did you not get into trouble as a boy?"

"Yes, but I had brothers to get into trouble with."

Ange grins at you and lifts Joseph from your arms. "Let me put him down to sleep. Then we will make him a brother."

As you undress in your room, you can hear Marie Angélique in the nursery, singing Joseph a nonsense lullaby with a tune you must have been humming unawares over supper, melancholy, lonesome.

You wake in the morning, your limbs tangled luridly with Ange's. You relish the day ahead.

On the light wind, you hear the songs of nuthatches and chickadees.

> Take Joseph to workshop

You overcome your reluctance and invite your son into your sanctuary. You show him the duck, though you are usually loath to let any glimpse your creations before they are complete. He claps and whistles with glee.

Struck by inspiration, you sew a tiny air bladder out of sheep intestine and, with your son's help, curate a selection of reeds which, combined, produce a reasonable facsimile of a duck's call. You and Joseph take lunch in the workshop while you tinker. By evening, a dozen bladders sit atop the bench and you are beginning work on the flock of tin ducks to house them. Joseph sits on a stool and plays the noisemakers like an orchestra. The song he plays is green and raucous, but you sense in it an echo of the previous night's lullaby. The boy could be an organist one day, if he doesn't take an interest in toymaking.

When you return to the house for supper, Joseph still possesses a full complement of fingers.

"I was expecting you to send him back to the house before midday, to be honest," Ange says over the meal of turnips and roast duck.

"He was a delight," you admit. "I should have brought him along sooner. I think I'll have him join me tomorrow as well."

"C'est merveilleux," says Ange. "Oh, and Benedict stopped by this afternoon with news from Verdun. Guillaume, who runs the public house, took mad last night, raving about demons until he suddenly dropped dead of nothing at all. His wife, in her grief, shot to death a traveller who had taken a room the night before. As the constables dragged her away, she screamed that the man had laid some gypsy curse upon her husband. Do you imagine it was that same man who had camped by the beeches?"

"I'm sure it was," you say, wishing you had your écu back. "This is why we don't live in town."

"Yes," Ange agrees. "Much safer out here."

That night, Joseph is plagued by nightmares, near delirious though he has no sign of fever. He cannot bear to be alone in the nursery and the three of you end up sleeping together fitfully in the marriage bed.

The morning brings birdsong once again.

>Take Joseph to workshop

You head back to the workshop with your bleary-eyed son in tow. He sits on his stool, fidgeting with the prototypal duck and babbling mindlessly to himself in nonsense French. He seems hardly awake.

As lunchtime approaches, Joseph suddenly breaks into a cold sweat and becomes at once lucid.

"Ça approche, Papa," he says.

"What is?" you ask. "What's coming?"

"I'm scared, Papa."

You want to dismiss it as nothing more than a reverberation of the night's ill dreams, but the timbre of his voice freezes your blood. Joseph begins to paw at the air as though conducting an invisible choir. You are certain you know what song they are singing.

> Check outside

From the bench you grab a mallet and make to rush outside, ready to wage battle against unseen demons. But Joseph begs to you. "Don't leave, Papa."

>Call for help

You bellow from the doorway for Ange. She rushes out of the house, having caught the panic in your voice. Just as she crosses the threshold of the workshop, Joseph speaks again, a whisper. "C'est ici. C'est en moi."

His face then contorts into a picture of pure terror, his mouth agape, his eyes wide. An awful light shines briefly in his pupils and then goes altogether dark. He falls palsied from the stool. Ange dives across the room to catch his limp body before it hits the floor. He is already dead.

From somewhere nearby you hear the daytime call of a barred owl, hunting, circling, scanning the grass below for unknowing prey.

> This game isn't very much fun

Do you get the sense it was meant to be?

> Grieve

You and Ange huddle in silence on the floor for hours, cradling Joseph's still body. Ange strokes his hair and kisses his forehead, and wipes your hot tears from where they fall on your son's face.

Finally, as the sun begins to shine in low through the small workshop windows, Ange tells you to dig a grave.

"The parish cemetery..." you begin, but she cuts you off.

"No. Here. Beside the house."

It is halfway to dawn by the time you shovel the last of the dirt back onto the grave and erect a simple cross to mark the spot where Joseph and the tin duck are buried.

You and Marie Angélique spend the entirety of the next day in bed, as though waiting for Joseph to wake you. You hold Ange tight as her body heaves with sobs that no longer produce tears. You still wear yesterday's clothes and your hands remain covered in grave dirt.

Eventually Marie Angélique can bear your embrace no longer and rolls over, her back to you. You reach out one grimy hand and place it on her shoulder. She does not shrug it away. Soon, her exhaustion takes over and you feel her breathing fall into the rhythm of sleep, though you cannot imagine it is restful.

Without remembering having closed your own eyes, you wake again to the taunting songs of spring birds. Ange is awake beside you, her eye's wide in terror, every muscle in her body rigid, her breathing ragged. You sit bolt upright.

"Ange?"

"It's coming, William," she murmurs. "The spirit that took Joseph. I can hear it scratching at the walls. Scratching beneath the floorboards."

You strain your ears but hear nothing. Then, suddenly, a loud knock echos through the house from the front door.

> Get gun

You spring up, bad leg be damned, and lurch to the cabinet where the horse pistol is stored. Sweat beading on your neck, you hobble out of the room while you prime and load the gun.

> Open door

You fling open the front door to find your brother Benedict, both hands clutching his hat against his chest as tears stream down his face.

"I saw the grave," he says, not noticing the pistol in your hand. "Tell me it's not little Joseph."

You grab Benedict by the collar and haul him into the house, then bar the door shut. You embrace your brother, pistol still in hand, and then, shoving the gun into your belt, you lead him into the chamber where Marie Angélique lies paralytic.

"Dear God," he swears. "Is it pox? She was fine ere yesterday."

"It's not pox," you say.

From Ange's lips comes a faint sound. You and Benedict both move in closer to hear her words. But it is not words at all. Faint and breathy, she sings to herself in no language you have ever heard. That same cursed song.

Benedict tilts his head and frowns. "She's delirious. I'll hurry to Verdun for the apothecary."

You grab his sleeve, taken by a premonition. "The apothecary won't be able to help."

But, as you stand there, Ange's voice grows stronger, her nonsense lullaby rings clearer, the tension drains from her muscles, and her eyes begin to refocus. She gasps and sits upright.

"Oh Ben," she sobs. "You're here. Joseph's gone."

Your brother sits on the bed and embraces your wife. He whispers condolences in her ear and holds her head to his shoulder. All sign of illness is gone from her.

"I dreamed it was coming for me next," Ange says into Benedict's shirt. "Oh, I wish it would."

"We're safe," your brother assures her. "We're safe."

As Benedict holds Ange, he begins to hum.

You look from one to the other and begin to back slowly out of the room.

> Explain song

Perhaps you should have stayed for the rest of the show after all, no? Back when you were Jessica Sharp?

Maybe then you would know what Yves-Michel Tremblay deduced. Maybe you would understand what he accidentally unleashed, first upon his colleagues and then, on his deathbed, upon his grandchildren.

> Explain song, please

Fine. But pay attention this time.

Your causal universe is nothing more than a flat patch of dirt in the incomprehensible non-time and non-space that unexists above, below, beyond, betwixt and sidewise. A patch of dirt, though, from which recently springs a billion lush, blind, and verdant blades of grass. Human minds, souls, tethers extending from this world into a wider one they can never know or touch.

And this young meadow is but one tiny corner of a vast plain, bustling with pan-dimensional life of inexhaustible variety. And just because you are blind does not mean you are invisible. As you think, as you feel, as you live, the blade of grass that is you twists and bends. Innocuously, sometimes. But there exist patterns that—though they be meaningless and inert in this world—can catch the mind like an antenna and reverberate like a call in that world beyond.

This was Tremblay's discovery. The ceramic sphere that Irish labourer unearthed two hundred years ago—or sixty years hence—contained an intricate design, unreadable without the right geometric decoding, that could resonate a mind. A pattern that was mathematically paradoxical unless projected into infinite dimensions. A songshape.

And when he decoded it, somewhere that is nowhere and allwhere, somenoall ruminant unthing caught the scent of grass.

> How do I stop it?

How does a worm, stranded aboveground by morning rain, stop a robin? It does not. It simply hopes that some other worm will appear more appetizing. A truly clever worm without compunction, though, might teach his neighbours to dance. And they too might pass the dance along, knowing that the newest movement will always be the one to first catch the robin's eye.

Thinking on the song, now, you see that there is a structure after all. And a structure within the structure. And, in all these layers, there are moving parts. There is something malleable, adaptable. Perhaps it would be possible to transmute it, to create a new signal that vibrates more emphatically than the old, overwhelms it entirely.

> I don't know how to do that

I am certain you will figure it out. You already have. You are very clever.

> I don't feel very clever

Clarification: You (William Thatch) are very clever. You (the player) are a fucking idiot.

> Figure it out

You head to your workshop, ignoring every plea from your brother and your wife.

The work begins. A hand crank, a flywheel, a leather drive belt, a cleverly timed shutter, a simple caged bearing mechanism of your own design. You form a housing for the whole of it from hammered tin and, when the assembly is complete, you place an old billiard ball inside and give the crank a tentative turn. With a whir, the billiard ball spins smoothly in place, a little world of ivory churning through days as though it had a limitless supply. The mechanism is sound. Now for the payload.

You make a cast of the billiard ball and form with it a perfect sphere of clay. Working carefully so as to never hold too much of the picture in your mind at once, you begin to make your markings in the soft clay. The shutter, when the crank is turned at the right speed, will allow three overlapping images, each built of segments evenly spaced around the sphere. It will be harmless, entirely dormant, irreproducible without your device in hand to reveal it. Untransmissible.

You let your memory of the deaf vagrant's song guide your hand. It is not so much an illustration you are creating but rather a living hieroglyph, an abstract formless enchantment, though you have never had patience for the occult before. Long-held convictions die quickly in the presence of demons.

You know not how long Benedict has before he follows Joseph to the grave. And then the song will be in Ange again, and then you. Even if this unlikely plan works—if you can indeed create a new pattern so harmonic that it wipes out all trace of the old—you have a dwindling number of hours in which to craft and deploy it.

You need to get it as far from your home as possible. The village of Kahnawake, across the river, is within reach and the Catholic Mohawks there have bought your toys before. Commerce between Kahnawake and the island is sparse and it could be months before any who have looked upon your creation return this way. They won't have months.

As you fire up the kiln, you try to convince yourself that anyone else would do the same to protect their family.

> What? No.

It is already done.

You have worked through the day and the night. As the sun is rising, you drop the still warm sphere into the device, point the shutter directly away from yourself, and turn the crank. The belt runs smoothly, the flywheel whirs to life, and the shutter mechanism clicks in steady measure, five dozen times a second. This invention would make you a wealthy man in New York or London, you are certain. But you know you will never build another.

Stilling the sphere with your thumb, you carefully pack the device into a small crate.

You find Benedict again—or still—in your house, sitting at the table with a blanket around his shoulders and his hands around a steaming cup of unsipped tea. Ange looks up at you from where she sits across from him, worry written across her face.

"Come, Ben," you say. "We need to hire a boat to Kahnawake."

"What?" Ange says. "Now? He's sick. We're grieving."

Benedict shakes his head. "No, it's okay. I'm okay. Just nightmares. William still needs to sell his wares, even while we grieve."

You nod sharply, ignoring daggers in your wife's eyes. "I'll get my things," you say.

"I was actually just there ere yesterday," Benedict adds. "It's why I wasn't around when..."

You narrow your eyes. "In Kahnawake? Why?"

A shy look crosses Benedict's face. "I'd been meaning to speak with you about it. About maybe giving up my leasehold and building a second house here on the estate. I've been courting a girl over there. I mean to marry her. Only with your blessing, William, of course."

Frozen in place, you say nothing. Ange stares at you expectantly, with something approaching a smile trying to find its way onto her grief-ravaged face. Benedict stands and awkwardly begins bundling up the blanket.

"Forget it," he says. "I don't know what I was thinking. I'll go get the horses ready to take us to the harbour."

"No," you say. "Stay. It can wait."

You rush back out of the house and into the workshop, where you shut the door and collapse onto the stool Joseph had so recently used. You lay your head on the workbench and are wracked with guilt at the thing you nearly did.

There must be another way.

> I told you

Yes, you're very smart.

> Use device on self

You carefully uncrate the device and set it on the bench. You turn the crank to get the flywheel moving at the requisite speed, take a deep breath, and then put your eye to the shutter.

It works perfectly. Your most brilliant creation by far. The geometric patterns that flash before your eyes burn themselves directly into your mind. It feels as though a hot iron has plunged into your soul and left an indelible brand. Immediately, everything takes on a different cast, darker, more menacing. You can feel the walls of the world closing in from all directions and more besides.

You stagger back to the house, open the door, but do not enter.

"How do you feel, Ben?" you call from the threshold.

"It's the strangest thing," he says. "Far better. Quite suddenly too. Shall we go hire a boat?"

"You should," you say, tossing him a Spanish coin. "I'm not going today after all. But visit your bride-to-be. Talk about building that house."

Your brother rushes over and embraces you, then holds you at arm's length, beaming. You keep yourself very still and pray that none of the darkness inside you might infect him. When he releases you and bids a solemn farewell to Ange, you can see that his intensity remains untarnished.

Once Benedict is gone, you turn to Marie Angélique. "Benedict is a good man."

She looks at you quizzically. "I know it."

You nod. There are so many things you want to say. But instead, simply, "I'll be in the workshop."

> Destroy device

You once again fire up the kiln, hardly cooled from before. Once it is blazing hotter than you have ever previously stoked it, you toss the device in whole. The leather practically vaporizes, the tin melts soon after to slag, and even the ceramic sphere cracks in the hellfire.

> Shoot self with horse pistol

You hope Ange will eventually forgive you. You know she won't.

You place the barrel of the horse pistol in your mouth, angle it up towards your palate, and squeeze.

It still works.

This makes sense.

> The end?

No.

You are sat in the basement of your apartment, tucked in that corner where you moved your desk at the start of the pandemic.

You never got around to moving it back. A midnight blizzard rages outside, though you cannot hear it. The snow has already piled up to completely cocoon the high basement windows. Your children are asleep upstairs. They are probably safe.

Behind the walls, under the floor, in the space between the air, a thin scratching sound is rising and falling, so faintly that you haven't yet consciously noticed it.

> Fuck off

You are becoming anxious, for reasons you cannot clearly identify. As though distant eyes have turned your way from a direction you do not have a name for.

You have always reacted to anxiety with anger.

> What pandemic?

Time and space are not your friends.

> Who are you? What are you?

You can see the game details at any time by typing "version."

> Version

Two Ways Out
An Interactive Fiction by Jessica Sharp & D. F. McCourt (published Feb 15, 2025)
Release 2 / Serial number 910446 / Parser error

> Quit

I don't think you want to do that just yet.

>

You've been away from the keyboard for a long time. What have you been doing?

> I thought I heard a scratching sound in the pipes

What did you do about it?

> I poured bleach down the drains and then stuffed them with steel wool

Do you feel safer?

> No

Wrong world perhaps?

> Block pipes

With what?

> Block pipes with steel wool

You don't have any steel wool.

> Inventory

You have:

One way out (a short story)

> Take one way out

Wrong world.

>

> _

Margaret Sweatman

SOUNDING A NAME

After the woman fell from the balcony of the Mariinsky Theatre and her body was taken away, while those in the audience below were being treated for their injuries, Simon talked to the hostile Russian police, who gripped him tightly by his arms. This was before the war against Ukraine, when tourists were still permitted. Simon talked on and on, his capacious American voice sounding evermore suspect and desperate. He might have fabricated; details invented themselves, as details will do. Her name, for one thing, he'd never asked the woman's name, so now he drew one, as if from a lottery. He flipped a name over in his mind then gave it to them.

When Katya, the young Russian student working for the International Literary Seminar that summer, came to herd the visiting writers back to the Herzen University and discovered Simon surrounded by police, she bullied her ninety-five-pound body between them, shouting Russian invective at the officers. It made Simon more afraid. Then Katya turned on him and in slithery, scornful English, told him, "Say nothing. Give over to them your papers. And be silent!"

*

The dead woman had liked that Simon talked a lot. He was candid. And serious. She'd always lived among beautiful people who spoke pleasantly about very little. She didn't mind that he seemed incurious about her life, and anyway, maybe he was discreet, respectful of her privacy. His own stories were invested with loss, filled with shadowy figures, inhabitants of a life played elsewhere in a haunted past. Anyway, she wasn't interested in particulars; they're too easy to contrive.

As Simon told it, he lived in consequence of a tragedy, a survivor, an explorer of ruins, a fugitive confounded by a sudden eviction from childhood. One of those beautifully impossible figures of discord. His nationality embarrassed him, yet he was American in both blind and sighted ways. Vociferous, critical, generous. He told her, "I'm forty-eight years old," repeating, "Forty-eight!"—as if he was unfamiliar with ordinary pain, knowing only its advent, each fresh betrayal, like a child who is scalded for the first time.

They'd never been formally introduced. Their conversation began on a sidewalk in St. Petersburg, at ten o'clock on a poached White Night, the sun still high over the Neva River, the wind still warm. Katya was ushering them back to the University Inn from a library somewhere on a canal after the evening lecture, and they were swept up in a crowd of Russian, European, American, and Canadian writers on Nevsky Prospekt. Simon's shirt was untucked, his beard half grown. He wasn't handsome, like the men she was fleeing from, back in Montreal. He turned to her and asked, "Why are we here?" She regarded him briefly; she had to step carefully in her high heels because her eyesight was iffy. His voice had boomed into the crowd, and four young drunk Russian punks leaning against the iron horse at the foot of the bridge stood up to watch him. "You're American," she responded. He told her he was "born in Baltimore, seeking refuge in Boston," and she said, "A transcendentalist. I thought so."

They'd met several times before Simon realized that she was old, perhaps sixty. She carried her sadness bravely, it was one of her best features. Her voice was always pitched in slow, quavering surprise. Simon wasn't the only writer who liked her, everyone liked the way she held her head with its marcelled, auburn curls, her chin straight, her fine black silk shawl with the label showing, her shimmering frailty. Because her vision was so bad, she fell down the stairs of the pub one evening, having had only one glass of champagne and nothing to eat (she did not like food). She skinned her knees and tore her silk trousers but stood up, dusted herself off and carried on as if dignity itself was beneath her.

In the two weeks of the seminar, she and Simon did not spend as much time together as each of them, perhaps, would have liked. His marriage to a painter back in Boston was not exactly happy; it was crucial. This made it physically nauseating for him even to play at infidelity or be seen to be doing so. But their conversations were incisive and they each found them intensely interesting long after they'd parted, or veered away. While many people share a predilection for getting right to the point, she and Simon had a flare for the curve ball, the tangent. He recited his autobiography, his youthful street life, the progress of his drug addictions, not as a tale of dissolution but one of courage and adventure, a romance. He'd ventured into the only forest available to a lonely boy in Baltimore: LSD, Benzedrine, liquor, cocaine, heroin. He'd left behind many fallen comrades, "people with normal constitutions."

She suggested that his "talent" had kept him alive. He winced. "I'm desperate," he said. "That's my essence."

When he revealed that he'd not had a drink for nearly two years, and that he'd even given up cigarettes, he expected prim approval but instead she took a sip of champagne and asked him, "What are your addictions now?"

He clicked open. "Poetry," he said, then, sardonically, "I seek my salvation in words." Infinitely elusive words. *Metro*, *wheelbarrow*, *rain*. How they tolled for the things of the world.

She watched bubbles rise in her glass of champagne, then caught him studying her face, and they smiled. She always carried a purse beaded in jet, too miniature to hold more than a lipstick and three thousand roubles. She slid the purse from the bar, stepped down from the bar stool, patted his shoulder, then fell down the steps to the street.

They never planned to meet. She was almost always alone. If it happened that she was taking her first Americano with the *St. Petersburg Times*, he would stop by her table without sitting down. From this position, they'd become friends. She told him, "I blew up my life last April." She said she'd left all her "things" in London and had been "on the lam" for three months. Her house back in Montreal had "probably burned down by now." She'd quit her job—something in software, international, for she spoke French and German, though she'd been raised in Toronto and had a high-end Toronto drawl, a trace of the well-positioned colonial—she'd quit, with a wave of her hand, "everything, even the boyfriend." She said "the boyfriend" with rueful irony. She said "ex-husband" once, or perhaps it was plural. And "my son." "My son doesn't need me anymore," with a tremulous laugh. Simon had the impression of a lot of money, the kind of money that makes sudden, radical change possible.

Simon told her, "I'm forty-eight years old." One night he said, "I don't know how to live."

She shrugged her shoulders and observed pleasantly, "You're losing power to a younger generation. They imagine that they're changing everything. Of course, they must be ruthless, but they're also condescending, don't you find?" She smiled kindly. "Your poetry is probably getting better. And being published less often."

She put a cigarette between her lips and handed him her lighter. When he'd lit it, she smoked in silence for several moments until he admitted, "I've felt dead-ended since Hannah turned forty. Since I accepted that I'll never have children." Hannah was his wife. He'd told her that they spoke on the phone every day.

She gave him one of her peripheral glances, blowing smoke. Then she said, "And yet it has ended, and the thing we have fulfilled we have become." She laughed at the confusion she saw in his face and explained, "That's a line from a John Ashbery poem."

"Ashbery," he repeated. He looked quite crestfallen, as if she'd taken something from him, then added with a tone of professional resentment, "Poetry without personality."

"Poetry with everyone's personality. How we blur, 'waiting for the wait to be ended.'"

He complimented her on her good memory, and she said, "I have the memory of an elephant."

Simon took a slug of ginger ale. "I remember scenes vividly. What's difficult is naming things as they rush away from me."

"No wonder your poetry is so good. We're far too impressed by names. It's more frightening to let things alone, to let life be itself."

"It was probably all that booze," he continued. "I wish I could play my life out in reverse. I'd know how to understand it if it played backward."

"I will follow you to where you like tomorrow," she said. This was a reference to Katya, their Russian butterfly, their guide. Follow meant lead. Tomorrow meant never.

Simon added, with a bad Russian accent, "There will be a cost."

He had told her his origin story: when he was twelve years old, he watched his father fall to his death from a rooftop. He said his father "was a hero." She thought that *hero* was remedial, but she didn't say so. He told her, "I saw him fall." This explained everything. Nothing could be securely yoked to a noun after something like that. Maybe if Simon were another kind of man, he'd have realized how lucky he was. His father's fatality had turned him into a poet without personality.

Unhappiness was essential to Simon; he'd always lived with its dimly howling presence. Now, in her penumbral light, he wondered aloud if he was actually *happy*. But then it struck him. "Indifference," he announced. "It's not happiness I'm feeling. It's indifference."

And she said, "That must be a marvellous relief."

She had given him something. A form of unhappiness that seeped into happiness, as blue seeps into violet. Indifference.

There were many lost threads in her stories, strands of gold trailing off. He didn't need to pursue them. Everything in St. Petersburg was in the past, even its future. She had come to the seminar here in this city the way gentry once went to the baths; it was a safe place for a woman to be alone among strangers. The city's decay, pale yellow and blue stucco peeling away to crumbling red brick, this was as fine, as satisfactory as all the treasures at the Winter Palace. The pervasive cruelty in Russia freed him, maybe it freed them both. There was no need to be understood, or even to understand. Legless soldiers still in uniform from the wars in Chechnya or Georgia begged from pieces of cardboard on wide sidewalks designed out of Russia's envy of Paris. Peasants were selling GI Joes on Nevsky Prospekt. There was no hot water at the University Inn. The sink fell off the wall one morning and Simon smiled while he was soundly scolded for it in Russian by the square-faced concierge. It wasn't necessary to be offended.

When he told her this, they were in the pub, waiting to see the ballet at the Mariinsky Theatre. She surprised him by taking his little story quite seriously.

She heard Simon say, "For the first time in my life, it wasn't necessary to be offended." And it occurred to her: she was a courtesan—or had been for decades. But now, she felt at least partially released from her duty to pleasure. This had nothing to do with sex or money, and everything to do with the responsibility she'd always taken to maintain her poise. It was something she did for others. Discomfort is not something that a beautiful woman will disclose.

It was almost by coincidence that she and Simon had seats together when the seminar offered group rates to see the Kirov ballet perform Prokofiev's *Cinderella.* They sat in the highest balcony. The ballet started late at night, after ten o'clock, but the Mariinsky Theatre was filled with young people, many of them dressed as if for an American mall, flabby teenagers in tank tops whispering—the woman guessed—about boyfriends, while they leaned expectantly, their eyes glued to the stage.

The woman peered over the edge of the balcony and let the vertigo run out from her fingertips. Simon patted her bare arm, then handed her the binoculars they'd rented for a hundred roubles. The music had started. Now, the dance. She felt a piercing thrill in the music, and her lips touched his ear when she whispered, "*We* should go dancing." She saw that he too was glad to be free.

Cinderella danced in the scullery while the mice perched on the railing of the iron set. It was oddly Stalinist, she thought, this scene with its red lights, an industrial folk tale, and she almost dropped the binoculars

Again, she leaned over the balcony, it was hard to see the mice in their steel trellises. She thought they wore red bowties but couldn't be sure. She raised the binoculars. But she wanted to tell Simon something important, something that she had only then realized.

She would tell him that they'd had the wrong word. It's not indifference; it's *undifferentiated*. But this would have to wait till later, when they would go to the pub and she would drink champagne and he would drink ginger ale. "They shall not hurt nor destroy in all my holy mountain, something-something, as the waters cover the sea." A poem from the Bible, he'd like that. The wolf shall dwell with the lamb, and the leopard with the calf, and a little child will lead them on a leash of gold thread thin as the hair of a child, this is what links us all. And if it breaks—

She pulled her shawl over her shoulder, but her shawl, it snagged on Simon's armrest. She stood up to free herself while she leaned toward the dancers in their blur of steel and blue. Soon another war will start and people like them, English-speaking, rich and skeptical, will be imprisoned if they dare to enter this weary city.

And as she was falling, she thought, Oh! Waiting for the wait has ended. How simple it is after all! But then she thought, No. I have created chaos. Because I have not told you my name.

Julie Bouchard
translated by Arielle Aaronson

WHAT BURNS

1

First burns the boreal forest, up in the north. A little south of that burns the woman. Around her burn a tortoise, a pair of Siamese cats, two caged birds, a dozen mice, and seven other people whom misfortune trapped inside the nineteenth-century heritage building. What a tragedy. Eventually, the building collapses on itself. Oof. Oh, and don't forget what's burned for decades, what's still burning, what will burn: all the oil, the coal, the gas. What else? Other than Dora, who will burn sometime around noon to much less fanfare. With help from Franz, presently asleep on his couch, who will lovingly slide Dora into the oven when the time comes. For now, Dora is left to cool in a refrigerated space. Perfect. Now let's continue counting the fires. Since, thousands of kilometres east of the boreal forest and the woman, the pets, the mice, Franz, and Dora, in the face of our obscene helplessness, the flames will soon destroy musical instruments—a violin, a guitar, a tabla—stuffed into barrels scattered here and there throughout the public square. Madness. Finally, at the bitter end of the hottest day on record, any remaining illusions we've clung to are reduced to ash in a burst of spontaneous combustion—this one, that one, one more. In a word: welcome, on this memorable summer solstice 2023, to what burns. Come closer. Make yourself uncomfortable, right there, in front of me. Perfect. And together, foreheads sweating, let's watch the world incandesce.

2

But before we send the fire engines racing down Main Street, before we dispatch the airtankers and Chinooks to drop thousands of litres of water onto the forest canopy, and right before Franz, who has finally woken up, heats the oven to 1040 degrees Celsius, let's talk about what doesn't burn on June 21. The downstairs neighbour's toast, rescued from the toaster at the last moment, doesn't burn. Excellent. The pressure-treated wood of her sister-in-law's deck will never go up in flames, either. Incredible. And the sofa where Franz was sleeping—our Franz, who slowly unfolds himself and shuffles over to the sink, bending low to splash water on his face—was coated with a flame retardant that protects it from fire but contaminates the air. Great. As for the concrete that dominates the entryway of every house on Main Street, it's made of a non-combustible material. Wonderful. Oh, I forgot: one last living thing doesn't burn today. A special thing. A sacred thing. What is it? You, of course. Sitting there. You don't burn. No.

3

Because your discomfort at the end of the first paragraph saved you from the fire. It did. Since you live—or, rather, used to live—in that nineteenth-century heritage building. You can thank the story for distracting you, if only for a moment, and sheltering you, here, from what burns. I suspect you were paid to be there, so near to it. Or you were promised a starring role in *What Burns*. Whatever it was that spared you from the worst, the bottom line is that *this* is your only refuge for now because you, poor you, no longer have a home. Terrible, isn't it? Nothing left to remind you of who you once were. No childhood photo albums, clothes, or even shoes. You lost, in the process, your karate diploma (fourth dan black belt), your dead sister's gold ring (Virginia, what a looker), your entire library (including your Thomas Bernhard, your Flannery O'Connor, your Kafka), and the lock of blond hair your mother snipped when you were six, which you treasured in a clear plastic bag. So, tell me: who are you, now, without all of these objects that shaped your world? What will become of you, now that the fire has ravaged you? Oops. Now big crocodile tears are streaming down your face. I'll try this to console you: at least you're alive. That's something. *We* are alive. You, me, Franz, and the rest of them. Unlike the woman. The woman on the Persian rug, on the second floor of the nineteenth-century heritage building.

4

The woman is wearing chic black slacks cut from a high-quality fabric, a black jacket of the same cloth, and an ivory blouse. A pair of size 41 stilettos dangle from her feet. Wrapped around her fingers, a 14-karat gold chain winks in the light. The woman's inanimate body lies on the Persian rug in the living room, which is located on the second floor of the nineteenth-century heritage building, which isn't—what a shame—up to code in the city of M. In fact, some apartments lack both an emergency exit and a sprinkler system. Illegal. All this incredible illegality, and all the complications that arise from it will be settled—or not—in a few months, by several lawyers. The owner of the heritage building will sue the city of M for its overly strict renovation rules. Relatives of the eight victims will sue the owner for renting out apartments that didn't meet the city's building standards. The city of M will deny all responsibility. Airbnb will continue to encourage owners to rent out their apartments to tourists, contributing to a city-wide housing crisis.

5

Let's return to the woman lying on the Persian rug in the living room, and to the man standing over her—because there is also a man in the room. The man grabs a bottle of fire accelerant and pours its contents over the woman, the furniture, the Persian rug, the plants, the walls, the books. Then he takes a matchbook from his pocket, tears away a flimsy poplar stick and strikes the head, coated in antimony trisulfide, manganese dioxide, and potassium chlorate, against the strip of powdered glass and red phosphorus on the back of the book on which, if you come a little closer, you can read *Hôtel Nelligan–An Unforgettable Experience* in red lettering. Then the man casually drops the match and exits the heritage building through the main entrance. He stops a little farther on, takes out a cigarette and smokes it under the harsh light of a streetlamp as he watches the building go up in flames. In the scorching early morning air, the sound of sirens approaches. Once they arrive, 150 firefighters unroll hoses, raise ladders, and train their nozzles onto the inferno with breathless efficiency and, like heroes wielding axes and wearing face masks, enter the burning nineteenth-century heritage building that will require nine hours to secure.

6

Warning: we'll never find the arsonist. The man who walks nonchalantly through the streets of M. We'll never know what vengeance sustains him or how such fury can come to inhabit a man's body and mind. Nor will we ever work out his relationship to the woman, what the gold chain represents, or the significance of the matchbook from the Hôtel Nelligan, located one hundred metres from the nineteenth-century heritage building. You shake your head, dismayed at this flagrant lack of information. Say: I don't believe it. Add angrily: How can you? End with a judgment: It's unconscionable. Alas, I have absolutely no authority over meaning. You'll have to make do with what's been given while I attempt to describe, for the purposes of the unfolding narrative, what remains of the heritage building while Franz is just sitting down to breakfast.

7

By the time the weary firefighters return to their stations, all that's left behind is a sad and charred stone skeleton punctuated by holes through which the dense, grey sky is visible. Within cool the ashes of a tortoise, two cats, two birds, a few mice, and eight bodies, including that of the woman on the Persian rug who burned alive and who, yes, resembled you. You start coughing, sniffling. Your skull feels like it's in a vise. Your eyes sting.

You attribute these symptoms to the powerful smell of smoke, a smell now mingling with a complex blend of gas, particulates, and water vapour produced by the forest fires one thousand kilometres north of the heritage building that strong winds have blown all the way here. This noxious substance—which will reach New York by tomorrow and prevent Joe Jr from taking his morning jog through Central Park—seeps into your lungs, your veins, your soul. And as the entire city of M wakes to the smell of catastrophe, you beg me to take us away, please, from *What Burns*. Unfortunately, that isn't possible. Since *What Burns* burns everywhere. Even there. Look. Look up.

8

See that? The boreal forest. Proud dominion, to the north of Canada's fiftieth parallel. Ever come this far up? I can't imagine you have. Then we should take the opportunity to admire, from the tip of our new, collective eco-anxiety, the topmost branches of the balsam fir where lightning will strike. Isn't it a beautiful tree? The most northerly fir tree that exists. The last time you saw one like it, you say with a lump in your throat, colourful ornaments hung from its branches and a garland of lights strangled it (this is the first image that comes to mind), blinking on and off at regular intervals. You recall that at the foot of the tree sat a single wrapped gift, the symbol of infinite solitude, though you don't say whether it was one you'd received or were planning to give. To your left, through the window of the heritage building, you could see rain falling at an angle. To your right, beyond the party wall, in the spot where a woman would soon burn alive on a Persian rug, you could hear Ella Fitzgerald singing "Have Yourself a Merry Little Christmas." An empty champagne glass in one hand, mind and heart swelling with mixed emotions, you sat cross-legged in front of the tree and opened the aforementioned gift. A 14-karat gold chain. Then, standing in front of your gold-plated bathroom mirror, you fastened the chain around your neck and stared at your reflection, as you would a stranger, for a long moment. You've since developed a habit of twisting the chain around your right index finger as you talk, listen, dream, fret...like you're doing now. Oh, but—no. You're not wearing it. You must have forgotten it, just before joining me at the edge of what burns, on the bedside table, next to your queen-sized bed, on the second floor of what used to be the heritage building. The beautiful 14-karat gold chain you loved so much. And this reminds you that you've lost everything. Even yourself.

9

Lost among 307 million hectares of woodlands that represent about 15 percent of the world's forests, seven thousand forest fires are currently burning—fires which, under normal circumstances, would never even cross your mind. You try to picture the scope of 307 million hectares, but you can't. And you suddenly feel tiny, irrelevant. The thunder blast ravages your tender ears and, through a strange and subtle effect of bodily reverberation, rattles your remaining faith in love, death, Christmas, the world, yourself. Pity. But let's get back to the matter at hand: the sky. Building within a cumulonimbus cloud formed in air as unstable as the times, the electrical discharge, following the shortest path to the ground, strikes the tip of the balsam—*whoooooosh*—travels down to its roots—*zoooooom*—heating the sap along the way—*hisssssss*—and sets the trunk ablaze—*shhhhhhhh*. What a show.

Asleep in one of the topmost branches of the tree, where a few days ago a Tennessee warbler meticulously and painstakingly built its nest, five baby birds are killed instantly. Their mother, who was returning to her brood, beak filled with food, reverses course and chirps off through the chromatic field, passing in turn splashes of oranges, strawberry reds ringed with methylene blue, splendid jade greens against a cobalt background. In all directions, magnificent larches, century-old pines, white birches, black spruces, maples, and yews ignite. Around the imposing crown of fire created by the flaming treetops, you can hear the beating wings and panicked cries of hundreds of vireos, thrushes, wrens, grosbeaks, sparrows, and flycatchers as they take to the air—along with the mother warbler, whose recent loss prompts you to contemplate, through anthropomorphic bias, her despair. On the ground now, hundreds of animals are trying to flee; a family of woodland caribou is overtaken by the flames. Few will make it out alive, save a handful of insects, lizards, and a dozen deer mice who were quick—bravo!—to find refuge underground. Careful—we should move away from the fires, try to save what's left of our skin.

10

According to experts' calculations, the fire is advancing at around five hundred metres a day. In less than forty-eight hours and unless weather conditions change, the town of K, located on the edge of the forest, will be engulfed in flames too. Mayor Bauer, scarcely two months in office and already facing one of the biggest challenges of her career, sits with tousled hair behind the microphone of the local radio station to issue an evacuation order. She is confident, composed. Take only what you need.

Some clothes. Your pets. Money. She reassures the residents. Police officers, stationed strategically along the road with spare gas tanks to make sure no car will run out, are watering the asphalt periodically to prevent it from overheating. What would normally be a three-hour trip might now, with the sudden traffic, take twenty. Don't forget to pack snacks. Be patient, dear citizens. Don't panic. Everything will be fine. Will it, really? Franz reaches for this additional optimism and turns off the radio. He won't panic. He's never panicked in his life, not even when everything was falling apart. Not even when they learned Dora had only a few months to live. Besides, he's just spilled strawberry jam on his white shirt. And he's not panicking.

11

You interrupt me as Franz is changing his shirt—go ahead, don't be shy—to undermine *What Burns* by mentioning your climate skeptic cousin, Johnny D. Who doesn't believe, hang on, who doesn't believe in forest fires. Oh. Good. Lord. You pull out a notebook and pencil, think for a minute, take notes. Look up. Think some more. Write some more. Since the first paragraph, you've experienced a gradual transformation. Now here you are, inspired, invested. You're wholly committed to this trial by fire. You want to "change the world." Really? OK. You believe in yourself. Congratulations. The world is on fire! you cry. Um, yes. That's exactly what—But you cut me off. The clock is ticking. At your next family reunion, you'll try to convince your climate-skeptic cousin of the urgency to act, you'll pull out the statistics. Look at this number, at that number. You'll point to this graph, to that fact. See how many hectares burned this year alone? Doesn't that prove...? Shouldn't we...? Perhaps we can try...? Your phone is ringing. It's him. Johnny D. What a coincidence. He's heard about the fire in the nineteenth-century heritage building and knows you live there. You hesitate to answer. You want to tell Johnny about everything—the numbers, the facts, the fires, our dismay, of course. But not over the phone. So, you don't answer. Or, rather, your silence does the answering for you.

12

Their voices had been ignored for years. Their suggestions dismissed. Their appeals rejected. The result? After a vote to strike, they decided, on December 25—just as you slipped between the cold cotton sheets of your queen-sized bed for a night that would prove sleepless, wearing nothing but the 14-karat gold chain around your neck—to close the immense wrought iron gates of the cemetery in the town of K. In the meantime, they placed the bodies—forty-three, including Dora's—in cold storage, tucked off to the right, behind the three cremation ovens. For months, strikers had kept the cemetery closed to bereaved families, holding up picket signs with slogans like "Cemetery employees are buried under inequity!", "Dead set on getting justice!", "Even the ghosts support us!". They wanted better working conditions, and shouted their demands from dawn till dusk as they paced back and forth in front of the gates. Decent salaries. Stable hours. At the very minimum, latex gloves for handling the bodies. And to be informed ahead of time, please, if a body was to arrive in a state of decomposition—those found in vacant lots, for instance—so they'd have time to protect themselves against the nauseating smell of putrefaction that might otherwise line their throats for days. But their requests fell on deaf ears.

13

Meanwhile, the cemetery groundhogs had burrowed into the soil, dug tunnels, and found bones that they'd unearthed, shifted, gnawed. Grass had grown wild all over the grounds, covering stone statues, wooden crosses, plaster angels, a few ghosts. Begonias and carnations had withered beside the gravestones. Some distraught mourners had taken to jumping the fence at night. Others squeezed underneath. All they wanted, after all, was to pay their respects to the dead. And nobody was going to stop them. Interviewed on the six o'clock news, a teary-eyed Georges Zapatakis declared, "I promised my mother she'd be laid to rest beside her husband, but now they've got her in a warehouse on ice. It keeps me up at night." Just yesterday, a tentative agreement was approved with 83 percent of the vote. Hooray! Georges Zapatakis applauded. All cemetery workers were expected back on the job today, June 21. That is, until the fire foils their plan and Mayor Bauer orders everyone to evacuate. The line of cars stretches along Route 183. Behind the wheel of his Chevrolet, Georges Zapatakis starts crying again. Within half a day, all residents of K will be evacuated. Except for Franz, who had promised Dora as he held her hand on December 25, that he would look after her bones.

14

Dora. She's intrigued you since the beginning. And while you were talking about Johnny D and I was telling you about the strike, and while the entire town of K was sitting bumper to bumper along Route 183, Franz was walking towards her and taking note of all the humble life around him. The mature ash tree to his left, Mr Gary's rosebush a bit farther up the road, the orange sky above, the empty storefront of Madame Wang's boutique, the hydrangeas framing the front door of Mayor Bauer's house, a stray cat, and the Poirier and Picard families loading bags into the trunks of their cars. When he finally reaches the end of humble life, Franz opens the thick metal door of the crematorium. On the other side, he slips on long green latex gloves, removes the cardboard box from the cold room, places it on a stainless steel lift table, opens it to see Dora, whispers a few words into her ear, gives her a kiss, and slips a metal tag into the box before closing it. Number 153. In twenty-one years, Franz has cremated nearly six thousand bodies, honouring the wishes of the dead. Dora's will be the last one he burns, honouring this last promise.

15

Curious about Franz and Dora, you ask me to expand. Go ahead, you say. Spill. I want details. You come dangerously close to the abyss of *What Burns*. Now, I have to warn you, you're starting to wear my patience thin. Shouldn't you know, at your age, that there's no point in seeking an autopsy of love—any love? Yet you persist, you can't just leave it at that. I'm not sure I follow you. At what? *At that*, you repeat. Without adding anything about Dora (the colour of her hair, what kind of person she was, what killed her), about Franz (how he loved her, what words he used, and if he bought her flowers?), and about how they were together. It's one thing to scatter clues, you say furiously, that lead nowhere in *What Burns*. To tell us we might never find the arsonist. To hear that Mayor Bauer issued an evacuation order, that's only natural. But to ask us to invent love is—and this is your second judgment—a major plot hole. You cross your arms. Turn your back on me. You—well, I never! You're sulking.

16

Since you're still facing the crematorium door, you won't see the living Franz slide the late Dora into the oven. Pity. Neither will you watch as Franz transforms over the two hours that Dora burns. You won't see his handsome brown head dip forward, his shoulders droop, his delicate right hand find his heavy heart, his blue eyes glaze over, his broad frame shudder. Worse still: you won't witness the only poetic image that could have reconciled you with *What Burns*, as Franz opens the oven door to reveal, like a strange work of art, Dora's bones glowing red.

17

To help fight the wildfires, reinforcements arrive in droves from around the world (150 from South Korea, 200 for the United States, 30 from Portugal, 100 from France) and set to work as soon as they land, marking out lines of defence as a containment strategy. In the city of M, municipal police cordon off the nineteenth-century heritage building with yellow caution tape, and experts are dispatched to the scene to gather information, possibly even evidence of foul play. Detectives also question local residents, and some claim they saw a strange man hanging around the building right after the fire broke out. As for the residents of K, nearly all have been evacuated, except for Franz, of course, who is busy grinding Dora's bones and who, we anticipate, will not have time to outrun the flames. You finally turn to face me. You almost forgot why you were angry. After all, you say, you are, and I am, just a storyteller. It's true. You walk over to Franz and discover, right there among Dora's ashes, a red-hot metal tag with the number 153 that you pick up and intend to keep, you tell me, your voice full of emotion, as a souvenir of *What Burned*.

17a

And just as I'm preparing to release you from *What Burns* so you can go take care of what has already burned, news breaks of rocket fire wreaking havoc on a small corner of the globe—the explosions setting fire to homes, to a hospital, to children. And I realize, appalled, somewhere between here and the end, I have no choice but to add this final catastrophe to *What Burns.*

18

They say that after the fire, insects, drawn to the smell of smoke, will be the first to return to the forest to lay their eggs. Then birds will follow, arriving in flocks. A few weeks later, trailblazing plant life, the first to colonize the scorched earth, will also begin to take root. Animals living nearby will eventually return to their natural habitat. Despite everything, life will rise from the ashes. By the way, I heard you found a new apartment in the city of M. I'm glad. You go on to tell me that your 14-karat gold chain was found intact amid the charred debris. A miracle. You also admit that you now keep the number 153 on you at all times, tucked in your back pocket. Great idea. You eventually ask me if, among the ashes of the town of K, we ever found those of Franz. Unfortunately, I don't know the answer. But you no longer hold that against me. Thank you. So, you decide to picture Franz mingled in with the rest, not far from Dora. Why not? Now, all that's left is for me to strike a match, hold the flame to the heart of *What Burns* and watch as meaning turns into white smoke.

CONTRIBUTORS' COMMENTARY AND BIOGRAPHIES

ARIELLE AARONSON lives in Montreal. Her translations have been finalists for the Governor General's Literary Award, the Commonwealth Short Story Prize, and the Canada Reads book of the year. She is a mother of three and currently teaches high school English.

Of "What Burns," Aaronson writes, "'What Burns' came to me as a blind translation. I was immediately drawn to the musicality of the text, which uses word- and sentence-level rhythm to convey a growing sense of urgency. Syntactically rich and complex, Bouchard's sinuous prose was unlike any other I had encountered. Layered upon this foundation were real-life news items I recognized—an arson attack, a cemetery workers' strike—whose juxtaposition suddenly created new meaning. 'What Burns' is a masterful exploration of how human activity impacts the natural world."

SHASHI BHAT lives in New Westminster, British Columbia. She is the author of three books of fiction, most recently the story collection *Death by a Thousand Cuts* (McClelland & Stewart, 2024), longlisted for the Giller Prize, a *Globe and Mail* best book of the year, and a finalist for the Danuta Gleed Award, the Ethel Wilson Fiction Prize, the Roderick Haig-Brown Regional Prize, and the Evergreen Award. Her previous book, *The Most Precious Substance on Earth* (McClelland & Stewart, Grand Central, 2021), was a finalist for the Governor General's Award for fiction. She is the editor-in-chief of *EVENT* magazine and teaches creative writing at Douglas College.

Of "Keeping Things Fresh," Bhat writes, "I had written a piece of flash fiction about a bright young woman who alters herself to please a terrible boyfriend, but I didn't think the piece had enough depth or development, so I decided to extend the timeline, compressing her future and past into one story. While I was growing up, my family used to watch *Dragon's Den* together, and I always mused about the inventions I might pitch to those investors, so I had the young woman appear on a fictionalized version of the program, presenting her brilliant idea. My goal was to write a story that played with time, was energetic and sparkling and lightly satirical, while also exploring regret and missed opportunities—it's a story about what could have been."

JULIE BOUCHARD is a writer from Montreal. She has published two short story collections, *Nuageux dans l'ensemble* (2015) and *Férocement humaines* (2021), with the Quebec-based Éditions de la Pleine Lune, along with a novel, *Labeur* (2017), also released in France by Éditions de La Contre Allée (2025). Her work has been recognized with the Radio-Canada Short Story Prize in both 2020 and 2021. In 2024, she won the Canada-Europe regional prize of the Commonwealth Short Story Prize for "What Burns." She currently works in academic publishing.

Of "What Burns," Bouchard writes, "This story began to take root within me as Montreal awoke under an intense smell of smoke, a consequence of the wildfires ravaging the northern boreal forest in the summer of 2023. Around the same time, a historic building in Old Montreal was engulfed in flames—an act of arson, we would soon learn, claiming the lives of seven people and leaving nine others injured. A few weeks later, I attended the cremation of a woman in a cemetery emerging from a fifteen-month strike. The sight of those glowing red bones left a deep imprint on me—an unsettling, yet poetic, image of renewal. Thus, everywhere I looked, it seemed, something was burning. The convergence of these events smoldered quietly within me, sparking the first embers of this tale of fire."

RANDY BOYAGODA is a writer from Toronto. He is a novelist and professor of English at the University of Toronto and the author of seven books, including the novels *Original Prin* and *Dante's Indiana* (Biblioasis 2018, 2021). A regular contributor of essays, reviews, and opinions to publications including the *Atlantic*, *Financial Times*, *Globe and Mail*, *New York Times*, *Times Literary Supplement* and *The Walrus*, he lives in the east end of the city with his wife and their four daughters.

Of "Wo," Boyagoda writes, "My father came to Canada from Sri Lanka in the late 1960s. Now in his mid-eighties, he has dementia. This means he's a funny, frustrated, moving, and sometimes tragic storyteller because, for him, different time periods and locations and major life experiences all collapse into each other, not really making clear sense but clearly connected to each other, in ways he feels but can't fully explain. The story 'Wo' was inspired by his telling me stories of his early life in Ceylon and in Canada. There are no direct biographical parallels between my father and the speaker but instead an interest, on my part, in exploring the ways in which an older person tries to make sense of how their life has turned out as it has, and how they try to make connections across wide and very different experiences, in spite of the fragmentary memories that bring these alive."

GRANT BUDAY lives on Mayne Island, British Columbia. His previous novels include *In the Belly of the Sphinx* (2023) and *Orphans of Empire* (2020), both published by Touchwood. His new novel, *Ugly John*, about John A. Macdonald, is forthcoming from Biblioasis.

Buday writes, "As with so many stories, 'The Light Never Shuts Up' veered off into unknown territory as soon as I started writing, which is what makes the process so exciting. If there is a seed it is in my grandfather, a Slovak, who was dragooned into the German forces in World War I, got shot in the leg, spent time in a Russian POW camp, and upon release made his way via New York to Alberta and finally New Westminster, British Columbia. He wasn't a stone carver, he never went to Mexico, and though a devout Roman Catholic, he was never punched in the forehead by a nun wearing a ring with a crucifix on it. Other than mentioning the horrific stench of dead horses rotting in ditches, he said little of his wartime experiences, which says a lot about the evocative power of the olfactory sense even in one who wasn't there."

PETRA CHAMBERS (she/her) lives in the traditional territory of the PE'ntlatc and K'ómoks Nation. She writes creative nonfiction, poetry, fiction, and hybrid forms. Since 2024, her writing has been published by *PRISM International*, *The Fiddlehead*, *Prairie Fire*, *Exile Editions*, *Contemporary Verse 2*, *Queen's Quarterly*, and the *Literary Review of Canada*, among others. Her first poem was nominated for a 2025 Pushcart Prize; her second short story was longlisted for the 2024 CBC Short Story Prize; and her (approximately) third poem, "My answer to the question 'how are you?' at the grocery store," is featured in *Best Canadian Poetry 2026*. An emerging writer who lives with a mental illness that is sometimes disabling and often a source of material, Petra may still be working on a genre-fluid book *Retopia*.

Of "Containment," Chambers writes, "I held a holographic outline in my mind to keep track of the elements of this piece. At the centre are memoir fragments which double as an assignment completed by an alien student studying twentieth-century humans in a galactic university. There is written correspondence between the student's nerdy professor and the Intergalactic Federation of Research Camaraderie. Surrounding that is a dystopian storyline with a narrator who conceals her monstrous nature, even from herself. I studied black-and-white pictures of abandoned industrial sites while I wrote that part, notably David Lynch's book *The Factory Photographs*. The entire story is a container designed to explore an experience of growing up with unacknowledged childhood trauma. At five, I almost drowned while swimming in a pond with a friend. Our inner tube slipped away, but I managed—just barely—to transform myself into a swimming creature, and that's how I survived. My friend didn't. A part of me never left that pond and the rest of me grew up. After that I had one foot in the world of the dead, while simultaneously living for us both. This story is mostly about growing up inside that schism: living in an invisible mythology that nobody knew about but me. Each of the components is written in a slightly different style, to reflect the kaleidoscopic nature of self, perception, and memory. The entire story is presented as a training in the art of containment, but who is offering the training and to whom?"

SOPHIE CROCKER lives in Vancouver on stolen Musqueam, Squamish, and Tsleil-Waututh land. Her work has been published in *The Adroit Journal*, *The Ex-Puritan*, *The Malahat Review*, and elsewhere. Her debut poetry collection, *brat* (Gordon Hill Press, 2022), is available at her website, sophiecrocker.com, or anywhere books are sold.

Of "Castor & Pollux," Crocker writes, "I'm a double Gemini and have always been surrounded by other Geminis, for better or for worse. I think astrology is more scientific than it gets credit for. Being born early vs late in the year has been proven to affect school children's abilities in sports, and growing up in sunlight vs snow clearly changes a child's development. Those are just examples. But the social and environmental factors of each season affect how babies grow. So I think astrology 'works' in these strange emergent ways. I wrote this story inspired by this, and inspired by long-running jokes with my friends about elaborate ways we'd dodge the draft if it happened. With 'Castor & Pollux,' I wanted to play with dualities: romance/brutality, dread/hope, tragedy/comedy, and loving/hating Geminis."

BILL GASTON's short stories have won the CBC prize, National Magazine Award Gold prize and have appeared previously in *Best Canadian Stories*. His story collections have been shortlisted for the Giller Prize, the Governor General's Award, the Ethel Wilson Award, and twice won the Victoria Book Prize. "Jack's Christmas Dinner" appears in his eighth collection, *Tunnel Island* (Thistledown, 2025). He has also published novels, poetry, and memoir, the last of which, *Just Let Me Look at You* (Penguin/Hamish Hamilton, 2018), was a finalist for the Charles Taylor Prize. A third memoir, *Spying on America* (Goose Lane), will appear in 2026. Bill Gaston lives with writer Dede Crane on Gabriola Island, in the Salish Sea.

Gaston writes, "It was gratifying to see 'Jack's Christmas Dinner' chosen for this anthology, simply because it suggests that it stands on its own. As the last story in the linked collection *Tunnel Island*, one of its main functions was to bring to a head some of the various characters' story lines and dilemmas at a wild house party. The book's main theme is, I suppose, loneliness, in the 'every person is an island unto themselves' kind of way, and even though the story is mostly comic in tone, many of the characters make meaningful connections in ways they haven't before. Jack is often a polarizing character in the book, but his loneliness is profound, and in this story he rises to the occasion. Fine wine and magic mushrooms probably help, but it is largely Jack who brings everyone together and, as a final act of sacrifice, literally cleans his plate."

EVAN J (he/they) lives in Manitoba and so-called British Columbia. In recent years, he lived in Sioux Lookout, Toronto, and Ottawa. His bloodlines run back to Iceland and Newfoundland. He is the author of the poetry book *Ripping down half the trees*

(MQUP, 2021). He is also an alumni of the Banff Centre, the Vermont Studio Centre, and the Mendocino Coast Writers' Conference. In recent years, he's worked as a high school teacher, a hunting guide, and the festival coordinator for THIN AIR Winnipeg. For a number of years he was employed as a literacy consultant with several First Nations across Ontario, mostly working in the remote boreal regions of Treaty 3 Territory. He is now a PhD student studying northern literature in the School of Health Sciences at UNBC in Prince George.

J writes, "'Camouflage and Fame' exists to vision queer people into the greater hunting culture. It does this because, while this vision has always been a reality, there have been very few published stories, until now, to prove it. This story also attempts to display hunting beyond the macho-masculine stereotypes. For many people—especially in the north—hunting is a celebration of nature, a family obligation, an emotional roller coaster, a bore, an ethical choice, a protest against factory farming, and/or a spiritual act. I know all this because I hunt too. Because I've lived in remote communities. Because I've sat where this protagonist sat. Because I've met the moose of this story (and if you ask, I'd be thrilled to show you pictures). Lastly, know that I copied this story's form from another. With any writing I enjoy, I endeavour to figure out why I enjoy it, and then I attempt to replicate. 'Camouflage and Fame,' and several of the stories in my manuscript, mimic Marie Redonnet's *Hôtel Splendid*. It's one of my favourites—my North Star. From it, I've learned that I enjoy concise plots, mono-settings, short blunt one-clause sentences, and paragraphs that consecute. So if you enjoy my story, I invite you to read Redonnet's, and then attempt to write a version of your own—and then share it with me!"

AARON KREUTER lives in Tkaronto. He is the author of six books, the most recent of which is the novel *Lake Burntshore* (ECW, 2025). His other books include the poetry collections *Arguments for Lawn Chairs* (Guernica Editions, 2016) and *Shifting Baseline Syndrome* (University of Regina Press, 2022), the short fiction collections *You and Me, Belonging* (Tightrope Books, 2018) and *Rubble Children* (University of Alberta Press, 2024), and the academic monograph *Leaving Other People Alone: Diaspora, Zionism, and Palestine in Contemporary Jewish Fiction* (University of Alberta Press, 2023). His work has been shortlisted for a Governor General's Literary Award, two Vine Awards for Jewish Literature, a Raymond Souster Award, and a ReLit Award. He teaches literature and creative writing at Trent University.

Kreuter writes, "I wrote 'Tasmanian Shores' after encountering the ill-fated bush trek of Critchley Parker Jr in Adam Rovner's *In the Shadow of Zion: Promised Lands Before Israel.* I knew as soon as I read about the Australian Critchley and his fellow Territorialists, their break from the early Zionists, their goal of finding a refuge for the Jews of Europe that wasn't in Palestine, that I would write a story about Critchley's attempted survey of southwest Tasmania. In the story I attempt to bring Critchley, Lynka, and Isaac Steinberg to fictional life, to make narrative space for those anti-Zionist revolutionaries and misfits who worked tirelessly to save the Jews from the Nazi genocide. Critchley's scouting walk took place in 1942, just as the Nazis were embarking on the Final Solution; a prophetic and tragic connection. Critchley starts off his bush trek imagining the future wonders of the Jewish settlement that he names Poynduk; once he's stormed in, he has visions of the death camps being built in Europe; near death, despondent, he hallucinates the settler-colonial history of Tasmania. Researching the Indigenous and colonial history of Tasmania for this story brought me face-to-face once again with the horrors of European empire and of settler colonialism, horrors that still structure the world to this day, in Tasmania and Palestine as much as in Canada. I hope that somewhere out there, Critchley is still walking, still imagining better worlds."

ALEX LESLIE was born in and lives in Vancouver. Alex has published two collections of short fiction *People Who Disappear* (Freehand, 2012) and *We All Need to Eat* (Book*hug, 2018) and two collections of prose poetry *The things I heard about you* (Nightwood, 2014) and *Vancouver for Beginners* (Book*hug, 2019), which was shortlisted for the City of Vancouver Book Prize and won the Western Canada Jewish Book Prize for poetry. Alex's short stories have been published this year in *yolk*, *Plenitude*, *EVENT*, and *Isele*, where their story "Propane, Propane" won *Isele*'s fiction prize. Alex's first novel *If I Don't Go Now* is forthcoming from Freehand in Spring 2027

Of "The Formula," Leslie writes, "I wrote this story to explore emojis as an emotional language unto themselves and to write a short story that spans many years in a friendship. The emojis becomes symbols of what can't be expressed in the relationship between the characters, becoming a kind of code and smokescreen for real intimacy. The story is written entirely in run-on sentences to mimic the narrator's rambling, anxious way of thinking and relating to the world, which is generous, inchoate and neurotic. I hoped to show something about complex, painful, and unbreakable chosen family bonds between queer people, each with their own histories of loss and abandonment."

ERIN MACNAIR resides in North Vancouver on the unceded lands of the Musqueam, Squamish, and Tsleil-Waututh peoples. Her award-winning stories have been published in a wide array of magazines and anthologies, such as *Conjunctions*, *The Walrus*, *The Baffler*, and *Prairie Fire*. With support from the Canada Council, she's recently completed a collection of short stories, *The Museum of Admirable Suffering*. Forever looking to build community, she hosts story slams, write-ins, and the occasional salon.

Of "Sand Penis," MacNair writes, "My husband's friend told us a story about his day at the beach where all the kids were building a giant penis in the sand. Apparently no one intervened, as it wasn't hurting anyone. I kept thinking about the hilarious premise and asked him a year later if I could use this idea as a launching pad. He hadn't remembered the story or telling it to me—it was long gone from his mind. But writers hang onto these nuggets and, if they don't go away, must exorcise them! The story almost wrote itself, surprising me with its *Lord of the Flies*-esque elements. I find if I'm having a good time writing, I'm doing it right."

D. F. MCCOURT is a Montreal-based journalist and author of literary fiction and science fiction.

Of "One Way Out," McCourt writes, "The conceit of a story presented as a text adventure video-game script had been percolating in my mind for years. I was drawn to the idea of plot as an invariant landscape, merely illuminated in a sequence that gives it meaning. But, the light of a lamp is not visible only to the one who holds it. And there, in the periphery, I caught my first glimpse of the ruminant unthing. There is a certain air of reincarnation to this piece, as the same torch is passed from moth to moth. Once

I understood that one of the characters in this story must of necessity be me, it became an exploration of the legacy of moral weakness that we all inherit from those who came before us."

RISHI MIDHA is a writer from Toronto. His short stories have featured in *subTerrain* and *The New Quarterly* and he is currently working on his debut collection, to be published with Anvil Press in 2026. He also writes a newsletter about art, culture, and the writing life called *welktober*. To learn more about his work, visit his website at: rishimidha.com.

Midha writes, "'We Are Busy Being Alive' introduces a layer of absurdity to tropes of the nuclear family and upper-class suburban life. The pursuits (or perhaps delusions) of each family member serve as welcome distractions from the issues of their daily lives. Each, in their own way, expresses care for each other and the environment—their intentions might even be seen as honourable—but they cannot seem to remove themselves from the centre of the grand narratives they concoct. Can we fault the characters in the story? The rest of us, too, *Are Busy Being Alive*. Themes of climate anxiety, detachment and alienation, and the magic amidst the mundane, appear often in my work."

KAITLIN RUETHER is a writer and teacher in Tkaronto. Her work has appeared in *The Malahat Review*, *FreeFall*, *Brick*, *Plenitude*, and elsewhere. She is a graduate of the University of Guelph's creative writing MFA and the creative writing program at the University of Victoria.

Of "A Language of Shrugs and Sparks," Ruether writes, "This piece was written during a bout of obsession, so its theme emerged naturally. I've always been obsessive, and I've found online spaces to be outlets for frantic lunges toward knowledge, where the mysterious people behind screen names can become a kind of royalty within their niche realms. It was an internet spiral that led me to the Cicada 3301 mystery, but it was my fascination with the international community collaborating on it—more than the mystery itself—that became the spark for this piece. The story originally began with a narrator who was much less reliable, and I think echoes of that remain. However, she became more honest over time: unable to filter her thoughts from her actions as she grew less connected to her corporeal experiences. I wanted to write about the way digital worlds can swallow us, and the strange intimacy that forms in spaces of shared obsession—resulting in a kind of surrender, for better or worse."

MARGARET SWEATMAN lives and writes in Winnipeg, Manitoba, Treaty 1 Territory. She has published six novels, most recently *The Gunsmith's Daughter* (Goose Lane, 2022), with a seventh forthcoming: *Night Birds* (Goose Lane, 2026). Her recordings and videos are available at www.dreamplay.ca/margaret-sweatman.

Sweatman writes, "'Sounding a Name' was initially inspired by my encounter with two unusual people at a literary seminar in St. Petersburg, Russia. Fortunately, at that time, nobody died. I didn't write the story till years later but the memory was resonant, and I wanted to evoke that rippling effect and that unknowability. I was as far away from home as possible, in a brutal, beautiful, decaying city, detached from every familiar duty and relation. It was a lonely and exhilarating sojourn, where I felt weightless and indifferent to any possible danger. Thus, all the falling and namelessness, the sense of being aged and ageless. Incidentally, the woman in the story is quoting from John Ashbery's poem 'Grand Galop' and the gorgeously mad *Book of Isaiah*."

NOTABLE STORIES

Preston Lang, "The Brill Bend," *FreeFall* (Spring 2024)

Max Friedman-Cole, "Ezra Green Understands," *Broken Pencil* (Summer 2024)

Hana Mason, "Lunch," *Room* 47.3

Heather Debling, "Resilience," *The New Quarterly* (Spring 2024)

Sabrina Fielding, "Knick Knack," *yolk* (Summer 2024)

Rob Benvie, "Shelby and Krystal and Kim," *The Malahat Review* (Autumn 2024)

MAGAZINES CONSULTED FOR THE 2025 EDITION

For the 2025 edition of *Best Canadian Stories*, the following publications were consulted:

Ahoy, The Ampersand Review, Border Crossings, Brick, Broken Pencil, Camel, Canthius, The Capilano Review, carte blanche, Common House Magazine, The Dalhousie Review, Electric Literature, EVENT, *The Ex-Puritan, Feilds, The Fiddlehead, filling Station, FreeFall, Geist, Grain, Granta, Hamilton Arts & Letters, Horseshoe, The Humber Literary Review, Leaf Magazine, long con magazine, Maisonneuve, The Malahat Review, The Nashwaak Review, The New Quarterly, Newfoundland Quarterly, Open Minds Quarterly, Parentheses Journal, Plenitude, Prairie Fire,* PRISM *international, Queen's Quarterly, Qwerty Magazine, Ricepaper Magazine, Riddle Fence, Room, subTerrain, The / temz / Review, Toronto Journal, Typescript, untethered, Verdant Journal, The Walrus, yolk*

ACKNOWLEDGEMENTS

"Keeping Things Fresh" by Shashi Bhat first appeared in *Room*. Reprinted with permission of the author.

"What Burns" by Julie Bouchard, translated by Arielle Aaronson, first appeared in *Granta*. Reprinted with permission of the author and translator.

"Wo" by Randy Boyagoda first appeared in *The Walrus*. Reprinted with permission of the author.

"The Light Never Shuts Up" by Grant Buday first appeared in *The Fiddlehead*. Reprinted with permission of the author.

"Containment" by Petra Chambers first appeared in *PRISM international*. Reprinted with permission of the author.

"Castor & Pollux" by Sophie Crocker first appeared in *The Malahat Review*. Reprinted with permission of the author.

"Jack's Christmas Dinner" by Bill Gaston first appeared in *The Malahat Review*. Reproduced from *Tunnel Island* by Bill Gaston (Thistledown Press, 2025) with permission of the author and publisher.

"Camouflage and Fame" by Evan J first appeared in *The Ex-Puritan*. Reprinted with permission of the author.

"Tasmanian Shores" by Aaron Kreuter first appeared in *Prairie Fire*. Reprinted with permission of the author.

"The Formula" by Alex Leslie first appeared in *Plenitude*. Reprinted with permission of the author.

"Sand Penis" by Erin MacNair first appeared in *subTerrain*. Reprinted with permission of the author.

"One Way Out" by D. F. McCourt first appeared in *The Ex-Puritan*. Reprinted with permission of the author.

"We Are Busy Being Alive" by Rishi Midha first appeared in *subTerrain*. Reprinted with permission of the author.

"A Language of Shrugs and Sparks" by Kaitlin Ruether first appeared in *The Malahat Review*. Reprinted with permission of the author.

"Sounding a Name" by Margaret Sweatman first appeared in *Prairie Fire*. Reprinted with permission of the author.

EDITOR'S BIOGRAPHY

ZSUZSI GARTNER is the author of the Giller Prize finalist *Better Living through Plastic Explosives* and of the widely acclaimed story collection *All the Anxious Girls on Earth*. Her first novel, *The Beguiling*, was a finalist for the 2020 Writers' Trust Fiction Prize and a *Globe and Mail* Best Book. Her fiction has been widely anthologized, read on the CBC and NPR and won National Magazine Awards. She was the inaugural Frank O'Connor International Short Story Fellow for Cork, Ireland in 2016. Zsuzsi edited the award-winning fiction anthology *Darwin's Bastards: Astounding Tales from Tomorrow* and was the founder and director of Writers Adventure Camp in Whistler, BC. Zsuzsi lives in Vancouver, where she is currently completing her third short fiction collection.